THE

PETTICOAT DOMINANT

OR

WOMAN'S REVENGE

THE

AUTOBIOGRAPHY OF A YOUNG NOBLEMAN

AS A PENDANT

TO

GYNECOCRACY

BY

M. LE COMTE DU BOULEAU

BIRCHGROVE PRESS

http://www.birchgrovepress.com

ISBN:
978-0-9870956-3-3

The Petticoat Dominant was first issued in 1898 by Leonard Smithers (1861-1907), an English publisher significant for his support of Aubrey Beardsley and Oscar Wilde, and his partner Duringe. It was probably published and printed in Paris, where Smithers' clandestine trade was based in the late 1890s. The name of the author, M. Le Comte du Bouleau, is, of course, a pseudonym. Authorship is attributed to an English lawyer, Stanislas Matthew de Rhodès (1857-1932), who is also credited with writing *The Yellow Room* (1891) and *Gynecocracy* (1893). It is worth noting, though, that *Gynecocracy* has also been attributed to the English psychologist, Henry Havelock Ellis (1859-1939).

The Yellow Room and *Gynecocracy* are also available from Birchgrove Press.

THE

PETTICOAT DOMINANT

CONTENTS

Avant-Propos

*NOW; I once saw the king who is Lord of many
people smitten on the cheek by Apame the
daughter of Rabsases his concubine; and his
diademe taken away from him and put upon her
own head, which he bore patiently; and when
she smiled he smiled, and when she was angry
he was sad; and according to the change of her
passions he flattered his wife; and drew her to
reconciliation by the great humiliation of himself
to her if at any time he saw that she was
displeased with him.*

Jos. Antiq.

INVASION

Chapter I

The Ball Opens

Happy's not the wooing
That's not long adoing.

Is an autobiography a mistake? I will first write mine and decide afterwards. Jean-Jacques Rousseau, the recollection encourages me, as is very well known wrote his Confessions—nice ones they were too—at length, leisure and in scrupulous detail and with conscientious accuracy. That is a fact to which I have recourse when I feel a want of assurance, as I do, not as unfrequently as I should like. Altogether, my aplomb, my conceit, my audacity or whatever you please to call it, I am shy and reserved, reticent, retiring by nature. I do not regret it, because women tell me I have a charming nature. Now an autobiography argues a sense of self-importance and implies besides that you can find no biography as well worth writing as your own.

Then too an autobiography must necessarily to a large extent partake of the nature of a confession, involving self-abnegation and denial, neither of which bashful as I may be, I can lay any claim to.

Confession makes one's friends as wise as oneself, discloses one's weaknesses, puts one at their mercy, one's non admission in the wrong, invokes pity, a near relation of contempt. Why therefore confess? Why not keep the secrets of the prison-house locked within it, show the world a brave front and never admit that one has either ever been, or ever can be, in the wrong, and then too I pride myself—*homme du siècle*, as I am—upon my consideration, for others' confessions have always appeared to me to be impertinent. They intrude an irrelevant array of facts upon the minds of others. I have always hated the button-holer.

What are his feelings, his experiences, his delights, his disappointments, his dyspeptic pains, and his aches to me? I have my own! And then it argues as already hinted vast self-esteem, self-esteem as hateful as Macassar oil; as hateful as oleaginous self complacency; offensive self-esteem. So in fine it seemed to me that I should by the act of confessing commit a worse sin than any I had to confess. Two considerations however weighed with me.

I consulted my friends.

"Until you have written your autobiography, my dear fellow," said one of them to me one day after luncheon at my club, "how can you possibly tell whether you ought to have written it or not?"

That seemed to me an unanswerable question. The other consideration was of a more transcendental description. It was the suggestion of a hypercesthetic apicius, of a nervous voluptuary who had not yet entombed his spirit in a living sarcophagus, who possessed mind welded or wedded in such a strange manner to sensuality that I could never hold any intercourse with him without afterwards laughing in secret on the first opportunity.

"Give" said he, "the melody of your passions, give your experiences to the world" (here a comprehensive wave of the hand included all Piccadilly, the Green Park and park of St James, for we were standing in the bow window of a club on the North side of Piccadilly) "to the world!" (both hands this time). "Those who do not like the tune will not dance to it; what is more they will be careful to produce another themselves. Your temperament, your sensitiveness much resemble Jean-Jacques Rousseau, follow his example; be like him also in this respect for all of us have to contend with woman. She is seven-eighths of the world. You have had unique experiences, facilities for gaining peculiar knowledge. The story you have to tell—your combat—will guide others." And then the rest of the society thinking me a little soft you know—not having "been in India; too much under the petticoat poor chap"—would chime in with talk about psychological studies and metaphysics and the anatomy of love until at last in the weariness of my spirit which I invariably find intensified by conversation with "My Friends" that is to say when they are "True Friends" or rather must be considered so, or better still so consider themselves.

I gave way; secretly however resolving to write for "Private circulation only."

Now where am I to commence? Preface?

There is no preface to this book. Also prefaces are written last.

My early years, my weakling, teething, vaccination, memoirs of the various nursery maids, I dismiss unrecorded: if the Faculty desire a narrative of this period, I fear I cannot oblige them; it would interest no one else.

One observation however suggests itself; if I was at that time what I am now, what transports of delight I must have received when gathered to the warm full breasts of the woman who bore me I drew from that holy source the rich and essentially feminine fluid which gushing down my throat animated my little frame. To men recollection is a life sickness!

This reminds me that from woman I received my life. I make my acknowledgements to her con amore. It is a sufficient explanation for my subsequent devotion. It leads me to reflect that for nine happy months I was inside and part of her; under her petticoats in a sense different from that in which I have many years been under them while outside her. A poet has spoken of this subjection as a reproach. I do not see why it should be considered as such. It is idle and useless to deny the vast control which a petticoat possesses. I tremble at the mere idea of denial. At one time it was otherwise but I soon learnt better. Many great men have gloried in the exercise of its sway, others have been compelled to submit to it. Was there not an

Emperor of the East, Michael somebody or other, the slave of two sisters, one named Zoe.

Achilles was educated in petticoats. In them Lydia preserved her Sybaris. Hercules and Omphale are like instances. Why mind the matter that for years upon I have been under their government. Looking back I rather like it. I differ from those heroes when glorying in a sort of emancipation.

I have often wondered how Hercules escaped Omphale if he ever did. No one has told us. It may have been my mere ignorance for at the end of my three years I coquetted with the enemy and was finally caught by her.

I open the volume of my life at the age of sixteen, when I was seated with an open book upon my knees in a room flooded with the golden sunshine of June, the open window of which admitting the soft breezes and scents of the summer flower-garden, looked out over an expansive bay spreading its argent and azure depths some two hundred feet below, and dotted here and there with white sails. I did not heed the treatise upon political economy which should have engrossed my attention, I was weak, delicate and over sensitive. The preparatory school for Eton had been found to be too much for my constitution. I had been recalled. My studies made subservient to the more important considerations of health, were not prosecuted with any vigour or regularity.

I dreamt with my hands clasped behind my head.

And my dreams were of the beautiful woman, a visitor in the house, some ten years my senior, who was arranging flowers in a porcelain bowl on a small round table near to one of the windows. Had I been older I presume I should have sighed for a younger divinity. Her age was just that to impress a boy. At any rate she exercised a profound influence upon me, and made an impression of which I am this moment still conscious.

Whenever I could do so politely, that is whenever I thought she was not observing me, I let my eyes rest upon her and drink in, as it were, her beauty. Every movement of her form possessed an indescribable, fascinating charm and grace—how elegant how admirable were its full round contours, how luxuriously, voluptuously moulded. I envied the flowers the frequent touches of her white dimpled hands to which they seemed to me to be sufficiently sensitive to derive fresh loveliness, fresh bloom, and increased fragrance. What exquisite mystery, pondered I, do those garments envelope?

Not knowing at that time what else to desire, I longed to press the ripe cherry coloured lips with my own, to repose my head on the full bosom, clasped by the firm round arms, feeling that in no other way could I obtain the satisfaction of my vague and indescribable yearning, and rest for my troubled soul. This would indeed cure my delicacy and fill me with vigour drawn from a sweet and inexhaustible source.

I therefore, wholly devoted my attention to the problem how to accomplish my wishes, and taxed my ingenuity for some circumstance which would lead to their fulfilment, without definitely evolving any method. By some unconscious cerebral action under the inspiration of the Divine Eros no doubt, I moved from my chair to a low couch. We had not spoken for some time. My movement attracted her attention.

"You lazy boy" she said in her mellow laughing voice. "You have not read six lines during the last half hour. You may congratulate yourself (shaking a finger at me with a merry look from her large dark eyes) that I shall not have to examine you!"

"Oh Laura" I answered languidly, "I do not feel well."

She turned to give me a glance of real concern. She knew no doubt what her presence was to me. No woman can be unconscious of devotion; and love when veiled attracts some women more than it does when, with the saucy boldness of Cupid, he sports naked before her. I allowed my book to fall heavily upon the floor; a little noise would create a sensation and secure her notice. I fell back on the sofa let my arms drop and pretended to faint. There was no one else in the house I knew well.

She was at my side in a moment. She knelt by me, placed her arm round my shoulders, caught my hand and held it, looked at me for perhaps a minute and them wiped my mouth, my cheeks, my eyelids. Verily I believe she had stayed at home to take care of me. I knew then her affection but not anything of love. Her warm form close to my own, her embrace her cool breath fanning my face, above all her kisses filled me with a strange and exquisite delight and I longed to respond. I dared not, she would have become aware of my ruse, and I dreaded her displeasure, for then, she could have been angry at the acknowledgement of her feelings made while she thought me unconscious, and we should no longer be friends. I allowed her to bring me round gradually, but when with a deep sigh I opened my eyes she instantly became more distant and let go my hand. I have often reproached myself with not having kissed her then. I believe I might have safely done so. I consider myself a laggard in love on that occasion, but be this as it may, all I ventured upon was to let my eyes speak for me, and press myself lovingly against her. She appeared a little astonished but there was a slight flush upon her cheeks which rewarded me by telling I was understood, as she leant softly over me.

"Are you better, dear child" she asked after a few minutes silence, "whatever made you faint? Is the room too warm? Shall I ring and tell them to bring you some wine?"

"No, do not ring" said I anxious to prolong these moments as much as possible.

"Very well I will not" she answered appreciatively "you will be all right directly" she continued, half rising to my great disappointment. "Oh Laura pray don't go" I cried looking at her significantly. "What shall I do for you" she enquired resuming her position and stroking my cheek with her hand, evidently pleased, while she pretended to ignore the state of my feelings. "Stay" rejoined I peremptorily. She laughed. "Oh! you must be good and allow me to arrange my flowers—or—or—or they will come back and find the flowers all about—and—and wonder whatever we have been doing." I again looked at her. Her coy conscious expression plainly showed that she feared being caught "spooning" as it was called at school, but I could see that she liked it, and I could not resist a superior, and I am afraid, slightly supercilious smile of amusement at her girlish weakness. "Yes" said I "provided you will promise me one thing." "What is it?"

"Say you will."

"I must first (severely) know what it is. You know" she hurriedly added in a sweetly reproachful manner, for I immediately looked like going off again, and she drew closer to me, "I will if I can."

"Very well then" exclaimed I, emboldened by my success and summoning all my courage to my aid, "let me come with you, to your dressing-room when you go to dress for dinner" and I looked full and boldly into her face. It was quite a schoolboy's notion. "Oh! Charles" she exclaimed with entrancing confusion, "you are too big."

I was I confess astonished at my own boldness and hoped I had not put my foot in it. I was shy and bashful. That is, I must have in excess for one of my sex that feeling which covers a modest girl with confusion when told she is a forward minx. Suppose Laura were to turn round upon me, I felt in that case I should die of shame, at being convicted of asking to be and desiring to be in a young lady's dressing-room during her toilette. The wish could only come from a reprehensible set of feelings. Will some one please explain why sexual emotions are ignored or tabooed? It seems so unnatural, so hypocritical and so contemptible. It was then with an exulting delight that I heard those words.

"Oh Charles, you are too big."

They promised so much. I knew from the way they were said, from her look and posture, there was nothing she could really like better than to have me in her dressing-room. She would probably have taken a keen zest in her sensations had I been able to force her to strip naked before me. I believe she would have thoroughly enjoyed being outraged and have much preferred that a rape should be committed upon her, than that her consent should be asked. There are women like this and they are always the most sensual, the most loving.

However my gratification and sense of relief in finding I had not caught a Tartar—whenever did opportune boldness with a woman lead to such a result?—diverted my mind from pursuing my victory properly and only left me with sufficient to punish her coquetry, it was the very fact of my being so big that made her want me—by rejoicing decisively. "All right, then you shall not go to arrange your flowers!" and I held tightly, with both arms in a freer embrace that I have ventured on.

"You naughty bad boy!" she expostulated, with delicious emphasis, "what" blushing, "what are you so anxious to come for?" "Oh you know, Laura, very well," letting my eyes dwell softly upon her and then travel slowly and significantly over her beautiful form, "and besides I have much oh! so much to tell you."

"Tell me now!" she whispered gently, approaching more closely as she yielded to my embrace. Why, why on earth did I not then kiss her lips and clinging closely to her allow my throbbing pulses to communicate the fervour of my passion? She would have been my friend at once.

Alas, I allowed the opportunity to slip and she was annoyed and justly so at the want of resource on my part; a total absence of resource as I did not reply even in words. Then came a sound of wheels in the distance, she thought the carriage was coming back. Looking at me somewhat coldly and slightly surprised.

"Very well" she said, in getting up and returning to the window—"Yes you shall come—you shall come." "You know," I said mischievously, "you promised you would give me what I asked if you could." "But what a thing to ask" she replied.

I did not appreciate this covert reproach and saw that her temper was ruffled. I should have hugged her on the sofa, tumbled her about, and fondled her, the ice would then have been broken. However I looked forward anxiously to the dressing bell. It rang at seven, dinner being about eight o'clock.

Laura was in her room, and thither I hurried. I quietly opened the door. She had already taken off her dress and I noticed at once with rapture her round white bare arms and swelling breasts. She gave a little startled cry as she looked up for I had not knocked. Her neck and face were immediately suffused with a deep red flush and she displayed her charms more by trying to conceal some of them with her arms.

"It is only I," I said, a little frightened; adding like a fool: "you said I might come."

"Did I?" she asked, a trifle vexed. "I have forgotten and—and so ought you."

"Laura," I said reproachfully, not understanding, "how could I?" "You ought to have forgotten," she repeated decidedly, with a smile, no doubt at my crass stupidity, "however you may go and amuse yourself with those sweets on my dressing table, while I wash my hands, as you are here."

I sat down by the table and gazed at her uninterrupted and intently. I was there by her permission and thought I might. She noticed and not with displeasure. I tried to absorb the beauties of her naked flesh her arms, neck, breasts and shoulders.

"Why ever do you stare at me so, Charles?" she asked at length.

I evaded the question, not knowing well how to answer it. Her short petticoat disclosed her well turned ankles and some inches of her slender legs. I longed to touch her.

"Let me help you dress," I cried, hoping it would give me an excuse for doing so.

"Help me! would you really like to? Well, would you like to change my stockings for me?"

I jumped at a suggestion exceeding my fondest hopes. She then immediately pretended that it was not seriously meant.

However I was not going to be done out of it

now and to her consternation announced my determination of keeping her word. She liked me better for it, and at last with much coaxing which she much enjoyed I induced her to seat herself in a low arm chair and abandon her legs to me.

I was in a transport at the freedom of the position and the opportunities it gave me of advancing my suit and at the same time of satisfying to some extent my curiosity about her hidden charms. Alas I know but too well now what women have under their petticoats, how often have I been kept there for their gratification my face closely pressed against them, unable to rise, until I felt perfectly sick, and then compelled by fear of smart punishment alone to perform what I came at length to consider the disgusting and degrading office of licking and tickling a lady's clitoris with my tongue. But I knew nothing of all this at the time of which I am writing. My hands trembled so much from the intensity of my emotion that I could scarcely exercise the privilege that Laura had allowed me. Half suffocated, my hands at length found their way underneath her skirts; and despite her pretty and mock resistance I uncovered her lovely limbs. The laces, frills, and embroidery of her drawers and petticoats filled me with ecstasy.

I folded my arms round her bare legs and pressed them alternately to my lips and then both tightly to my face and breast. I kissed her feet. I endeavoured to kiss her legs above the knee. She gave me a stinging slap. It served only to increase my fervour. I seized her in my arms and covered her face, her eyes, her mouth, her nostrils with passionate burning kisses, then I let my head descend to her bosom, I swallowed in her naked breast, I kissed them, licked them, bit them, filled my mouth with their soft flesh, and rose coloured nipples. Laura was startled, perhaps a little frightened at my violence. Presently I found myself in some inexplicable way between her legs lying in her lap—a fresh and strange madness took possession of me, and it seemed of Laura also, for she kissed me back. Beside myself, I threw away all restraint, I endeavoured with my hands to remove her clothes and unfastened my own. My hand slipped up to her body. What was it, wet soft and hairy, that I had touched?

The moment I had touched it—and I had done so accidentally, after all—she was suddenly transported with anger.

"How dare you?" she demanded in a low furious tone, "how dare you?—Go away. I will have you whipped." And she sprang up. The word thrilled me oddly. I found myself overwhelmed with confusion kneeling at her feet. She would not let me put her stockings on. I pined to touch her slender limbs again.

I begged for forgiveness; with much ado and reluctantly she permitted me to touch her hand with my lips, more I could not obtain. Her manner was entirely changed and all my entreaties failed to restore her kindness.

During the evening her coldness grew more and more marked. The next day I was informed (Laura must in the interval have had a conversation with the authorities) that I was to be sent to Holywell Hall where some cousins were being educated by a clever and very accomplished French governess. It was, I was told, by far the best place for me; and the hope was expressed that there, under the tender care of the lady alluded to, my studies would really make some progress.

The care of the lady made me tender indeed.

I had not the happiness before I started of seeing Laura again. I tried to, for her conduct was an inexplicable enigma. While lying in her lap—how exquisite the recollection—she had kissed me, given me my kisses back, and shown more than one indisputable sign of enjoyment at my being there. Why did she wish to disguise the fact now? What had transformed her favour into animosity?

I had reluctantly to depart, without the much desired explanation, in ignorance.

But now I understand that ladies loved to be wooed.

I had been too precipitate, too brave, and at the wrong moment.

Chapter II

Vicissitudes of the Struggle

Let the play begin!
The Rebecks are in tune.

The Devil take it! The idea of being packed off to a governess. The idea at my age of such a thing being possible! It did not commend itself to me at all. My feelings I remember defied analysis, at this distance of time I have to collect myself in order to describe them.

Being packed off to a governess! a governess! it was an indignity, a humiliation, and disparagement of my native worth, a diminuation of the importance and invasion of the prerogative of my sex. Was I not bound to resist as a representative of male humanity?

For what might not craven submission render me responsible? A governess! A thing, a female thing in petticoats to order me about, to restrain me with her petty views and puerile, feminine discipline! The mere idea, apart from the reality, made me wild with indignation, gave me a keen sense of abasement. But the secret consciousness of my impotence made me sick.

Laura! Laura! what a cruel return. What a mean advantage to take of my susceptibility which had become known to you in the intimacy of the intercourse you yourself permitted. I testified my devotion towards you in a manner that was at once natural and masculine.

If it was precocious would you have had me less than a man? would you, as a woman have wished me to desire and seek less, or otherwise than I did.

You should have gloried in my devotion. Why were you not true to yourself? You had precedents for it.

Henry VIII sent "Mr Peter Aretine the right naturel poet" three hundred gold crowns; Edouard VI's clerk of the Closet, William Thomas, a prebendary of St Paul's, addressed a dedicatory letter by that title, to the earnest fellow; the Emperor Charles V rode with him on his right hand in intimate conversation; Pope Julius III presented him with a thousand gold crowns and a knighthood, a dignity to which an annual income was attached to boot. Was I less deserving of reward than Pietro Aretino? Was I also to suffer because I sought reward at the hands of a woman, at your hands? Had I written naughty verses and made worse pictures, and vicious books? Why should he for being natural receive gold crowns and favours from Emperors and kings, and compliments from Ecclesiastical dignitaries, and I be packed off to a Governess? How you failed to appreciate, instigated by some detestable pruriency, by some ridiculous and affected prejudice, devotion and human nature! How you failed to appreciate me. None could have been more sincere, more true. And simply because I accidentally touched a secret portion of your frame, and I suppose awakened passions which terrified you, simple girl! Do you wish me indeed to grow up useless, weak, impotent, by seeking to have me educated like Charles VIII of France amongst low and effeminate people? In calmer intervals, the matter assumed another aspect. I consoled myself by other historical instances. As an homme du siècle, I finally thought the notion bizarre and I laughed. It was a notion of which much might be made. After all I should manage to escape without any serious compromise. My experience my manhood the greater weight would inevitably as a consequence tell in the end. I should gain an undoubted ascendancy. I must in the end, by mere specific gravity, defeat Laura and her fell cruel and ungrateful designs for which she deserved to live and die an old maid.

We, Mademoiselle and I, would be very good friends. After all what could she do? She would know, or at least could soon learn, the only possible mode of treating a person of my age and sex, she could sympathise with me, we should rise against the common enemy, and Laura's plans would be put to ridicule.

I had a great respect for myself and no small opinion of what was due to me. Mademoiselle would know her proper place, and quickly discover her level.

I had heard she was a "blue," she no doubt with awe and trembling would suggest a little Homer, or a little Virgil, and we would laugh together over Horace.

Lucretius and Martial and Petronius I should have to read alone—I should have my own rooms, my own amusements, my guns, my dogs, my fishing rods.

The uncertain readings of the text would be determined by me with the aim and accuracy of a doctor, and my decision accepted as final. The girls would regard me as a hero, as a being whose goings and comings were beyond their control, as an enigma whose vagaries were ascribable to and to be explained only by the sacred mystery of his sex.

If I came home at midnight I should have been simply exercising my recognised privileges. They would descend in their dainty night robes, or peignoirs, and let me in, and with admiration and say: "Oh! it was only Charles returned from fishing or from supper after a long day's shooting." And all would be regular and in order and I would excite most envy in the feminine bosoms and be the close ally and confidant of Mademoiselle, and derive a vast increase of self-respect from it all.

I had uncertain and hazy visions too, of the possibility of the existence of farmer's daughters on the estate. Clear visions of moonlight nights, with pretty frightened figures at garden gates, of soft beautifully moulded hands against my lips, and buxom forms palpitating upon my own with the emotions I had inspired, haunted and excited my fancy. I dreamt of frolics with the merry milkmaids and some joke about behaving to them as they treated their cows amused me for twenty four hours.

But it is true that with the farmer's daughters when I had caught them, I was quite at a loss to know what I should do.

At other moments again I bitterly reproached Laura for having had me sent to a governess, because I attempted to fondle her at a moment in which in the innocence of my heart, I thought she would delight in it.

I believe her resistance was pure affectation instigated by a fear of losing prestige. I flushed with shame when I reflected how fine, how spirituelle, her revenge was. I had discovered my weakness to her, and I could not get rid of an acute sense of wrong at the ungallant advantage she had taken of it. What an outrage to put me under those very petticoats she knew that I found irresistible. How cruel in addition to thus delicately and tacitly signify her disbelief that my devotion was to her individually. What a slew upon my virility. She should have instinctively felt that I was more than man enough to allow myself to be the slave of petticoats, unless worn by her. This feeling was intensified by a tacit acknowledgment of the shrewdness of her perception. She was right, she saw through me, but I could not own it even to myself. Any petticoats I feel I was constitutionally bound to worship, still she ought not to have known this or knowing it, the confidential character of the mode in which she had found it out, should have precluded her recognition of the fact and her availing herself of it to punish me. It was a mean suspicion which nothing could justify. I would now show that a tutor at least and not a governess was what the case demanded.

In my soul I rather quivered with carefully concealed delight that it was a governess—as I have said, it promised so many possibilities of pleasure. But this did not justify her. My Father, an Earl, had five chaplains, most of them beneficed clergymen. I should have been sent to one of them. Clergymen's daughters (they invariably have daughters) are always fine, waggish, rakish and up to date young ladies, and as I was the eldest son of their patron, Lord Linwood, I would have cut a fine figure with them. In the natural course of events this is what could have happened. But Laura had interfered with the natural course of events. It was all owing to her I felt convinced that instead I was sent to Holywell Hall, her doing that put me under the charge of Mademoiselle Diane d'Erébe, on a level with my cousin Barbara, a mere feminine child of nineteen.

How singularly *mal-apropos*, what a pathetically ignorant indifference to the demands of that gallant disposition of which but for her own folly I was about to give her a convincing proof after my own manly fashion; how little respect she showed for a young man of my age. It astonished!

The resolution that I formed however resembled Shylock's. I determined to profit by the instruction so that if it ever came to her knowledge it would cause her, deservedly, infinite chagrin.

Well, I had been perhaps three days at Holywell Hall, cutting a splendid figure half flirting with Mademoiselle, and establishing with Barbara a character absolutely heroic. At night retiring with éclat to my room, having as I supposed made the women (I call them girls) as envious as any man could wish and there secretly smoking in what I considered as an inviolable sanctuary, when there came a rude awakening; a positively rude awakening such as I could not possibly have anticipated.

Holywell Hall is a large and old fashioned mansion. Some heiress or other brought it into the family. About one third only I found was in actual occupation. It stood in a large park in the heart of the country, and was the principal seat of the midland country in which it was situated. It was but little visited as the Earl's absence was generally known.

He possessed so many Castles, Courts and Halls that to live in them all was an impossibility. Mademoiselle Diane d'Erébe was a fine tall girl of eight and twenty. So demure, so stately, so scornful, so exquisitely beautiful.

Governess indeed!

The flame in her eyes, I think, first scorched me. Her low brow about which the dark hair clustered in thick and glossy ringlets was a dream in itself, of loveliness. Her square figure and well set up shoulders gave an indication of power which to a susceptible being like myself were very embarrassing.

Her complexion was of lily whiteness and formed a surprisingly striking and admirable contrast with her black hair. About her movements there was pretty precision and wilfulness which effectually ostracised the possibility of questioning her wishes.

Barbara, well Barbara was just budding into womanhood, and was just my size. I need not trouble myself or the reader with a description of Barbara; forward minx!

"Wait for me here, Master Charles at twelve o'clock" said Mademoiselle, one fine morning with an air of severity she had not before permitted herself to use to me. She had actually given me, Me, some French themes to do in one of Allen's Elementary French books, such a puerile employment for a young man of my calibre, and I had been toying and playing with them ever since a quarter to eleven at which hour, instead of half past nine the right one, I had condescended to enter the school-room.

Alas! it should have been Aeschylus or Sophocles or Dante, or Boccacio or Theophile Gaultier at the least: Alas! she was making a fool of me! Making me ridiculous in the eyes of Barbara, of herself, and above all in my own: I have no doubt that I have the reader's entire sympathy.

I had understood she was educating cousins. But Barbara was the only one I had. Some other young ladies it is true came in but for some inexplicable reason Mademoiselle had dis-missed them constantly during those first three days.

Twelve o'clock arrived, and Mademoiselle and Barbara left the room but I was not allowed to do so.

I hummed and hawed. It was inconvenient.

I had arranged with one of the under keepers to go to the lake at half past twelve to catch some of the famous lazy tench that came to the surface of its waters in the hot afternoon, with a delicate line attached to a tiny hook, or failing that to shoot them with a small-bore rifle. Both methods are good sport as I who had shot grey and red mullet in rocky pools in the southwest of Ireland in my time knew very well.

This delay was inconvenient. I walked up and down. Ten minutes past twelve—a quarter past—twenty past. I should be late.

I could not get to the lake in time. The man would think I was not coming, I could not manage the punt and the fishing tackle alone. My afternoon's sport would be spoilt. What could Mademoiselle want? Why should I wait for her? At twenty five minutes past (what right had she to keep me) I resolved I would not wait any longer, I would go.

I marched up to the door with manly determination and defiance. It was locked; she had turned the key outside.

I became mad with rage. I kicked a chair over, threw some books about, stuck my thumbs in the arm holes of my waistcoat and marched about furiously. This was some silly tick of Barbara's.

How dared she? I would teach her to play such tricks on me! In the midst of my anger the door opened quietly and in walked Mademoiselle in a simple, severe, classical princess robe in which she looked very stately, very majestic. There was a look of quiet amusement in her large dark eyes.

"Oh Mademoiselle," I cried, hesitating as I scanned and stopped to admire her toilette, "I am going to fish. I arranged to meet Hobbs at half past twelve. Do speak to me another time, or I shall be too late!"

"You cannot go fishing this afternoon, I cannot allow it, you have had too much freedom as your behaviour has proved."

I looked at her in amazement. She quietly seated herself. "Kneel down!" she continued, pointing to the ground at her feet and looking full at me.

"Kneel down!" I echoed, stupefied.

"Yes; kneel down there and put your hands behind you."

"What joke — what nonsense — what tom-foolery. . ." I began as, to humour her, and half dismayed and frightened, I set about obeying.

"Joke — nonsense — tom-foolery — are these words to use to me?" She asked looking down very seriously at me.

I was too startled to say anything and looked up at her with blank astonishment.

"To me, your governess!" she went on, moving her feet. I still looked at her.

"Tiens!" she said, as she proceeded to smack my face four or five times vigorously before I could spring up. Almost in tears from the tingling and the ignominy, I stood some yards off, trying to collect my scattered senses, scarcely able to believe in the reality of what she had done.

She rose, she was a tall girl, how my feelings bubble and boil while I write this of a girl, how my blood boils! She was a tall girl, taller than I; she rose, walked over to me, and caught me by the left ear, pinching it dreadfully.

Without a word she marched me out of the room, along the corridor to her own bedroom. She set me free with a stroke and locked the door.

"Now I will give you a lesson," she observed.

"Take off your jacket and waistcoat."

Having given me this order she walked to a chest of drawers and opening one took out a slender riding whip which she regarded with

complacent satisfaction and then negligently
threw on a couch. Then she looked in two or
three drawers for something she could not
readily find. At last with a little exclamation of
triumph she unearthed what appeared to me to
be two web garters with silver rings stitched
into them and what I should have imagined to
be a small bag handle with spring catches at
each of its ends.

"Why have you not taken off your jacket and
waistcoat?" asked she pausing menacingly with
one of the garters in her hands.

"Take them off instantly or—" and she picked
up the whip.

I did not at all like it but considered a little
complaisance most politic under the circumstances, it would be an awful thing if she were
driven to the rudeness of striking me, whatever
feelings a jewelled riding whip in her hands
might produce.

So I looked at her, and at the dainty whip in
her dimpled hand, and at her flashing eyes.

After all it was but my waistcoat and jacket
which I was invited to remove. The strangeness
of the order and the difficulty because of the
self-abnegation involved in complying gave it a
certain zest undoubtedly. Mademoiselle was of
such surpassing loveliness and her wilfulness
was so pretty and becoming that it was
charming to be ordered about by her while her
tyranny was thrilling and delightful. I really
could not count myself altogether unfortunate
to be so thoroughly taken in hand by her. Still it
was a very novel experience to be thus at the
mercy of a girl, in her own bed-room too. It

seriously compromised my dignity and made me feel very small. But there she stood firm determined and impatient as these ideas flashed through my mind. No doubt, if I hesitated longer I should have that whip about my shoulders.

The idea in her graceful presence cowed me. At last, I resolved to obey, but as I did so was careful to mark by a certain petulance in my manner that I considered that really quite too much was being required of me and that the joke might be carried too far.

Mademoiselle noted this little air of annoyance; and an amused and satirical smile played about the corners of her delicately curved mouth.

The moment I had cast the two garments aside, she promptly walked up to me and without a word or making any fuss about it seized my right arm with a firm strong grip and tightly buckled one of the garters on to it, outside the shirt-sleeve and above the elbow. She then sharply snipped into its ring the spring hook at one of the ends of what I have named the bag handle, in reality a vixenish contrivance for fixing the elbow and with it the whole arm. That done, she pounced on the other arm forcibly held it having without any ceremony pulled me round while she tightly adjusted the second garter upon it.

Then still grasping the same arm with her left hand and catching the bag-handle with her right she pulled and jerked my elbows together at the back. I cried out, so violent was she, that she could break the bones but she did not heed me in the least—until she succeeded after some violent exercise in snipping the still free hook into the other vacant ring. When she had accomplished this I was securely pinioned. The handle was but three and a half or at the most four inches long and my chest was a somewhat contracted one and I was thus unable to make any effective use of my hands and arms. I was painfully fixed and my shoulders already ached from the strain. My exclamations and protests, my restlessness and anger, under the confinement she inflicted only seemed to excite her mirth as she contemplated with triumphant satisfaction and with huge and undisguised delight the predicament I was in. I felt hurt. I thought she might have shown a little feeling instead of this indecent joy, or have at least concealed it. After a moment or two, standing beside me with her hand upon my shoulder, she smilingly said: "Now walk across to my bed." Some what annoyed at her peremptoriness I allowed myself to be half pushed half led to it. To my amazement she placed me with my back to its side and with both hands upon my shoulders facing me forced me face uppermost on to it. She then leant over me with her arm pressed down across my chest to prevent my rising, and seated herself on the edge so close to my side that I felt oppressed by her weight, her feet dangling on the floor she began lecturing me.

"Master Charles.

"So even at your tender age, you have developed a liking for being in young ladies' dressing-rooms—yes—I know all about it from

Miss Laura who is a particular friend of mine—my cousin in fact."

I was horrified.

"Yes, you may thank your stars that no worse fate has befallen you in consequence of the liberties you attempted to take with her, than falling into my hands.

"Lie still! How did you feel when you were that night in her lap and she was *en deshabille* and had even allowed you to take her stockings off, and you attempted a gross liberty with her in return for the favour. You see, I know all.

"Had you any sensations here for instance" asked Mademoiselle freely passing her hand down over my abdomen and between my legs. "What, you will not own to them! Well we shall see presently—and then you pretended to faint to coin kisses, wretched young man—kisses, like this and this," turning and pressing her form and breast against mine as she kissed my lips and in the most abandoned fashion put her legs across my own.

"Yes they are nice, aren't they! and it is nice to be under my lap, I dare say, but all to be dearly purchased—no love, no true love inspired them—yours were only brutal passions, the seat of which is here" viciously pressing and pinching my virility and not stopping at that, but slipping down her hand pushing it right through between my crossed legs, and pinched me vigorously saying: "and here." She disconcerted me terribly, so did her next sentence.

"I will make it smart presently. I promise you. Laura did not know how to punish you! I do.

Your bare bottom shall be at my mercy soon, and you will speedily implore grace with tears and abject entreaties, I know how to treat a precocious boy, Master Charles; that is why you have been sent to me."

"I am not Master Charles, I am Lord Linwood" and blushing fiery red "do you think you will whip me, you immodest girl?"—I struggled under her weight. "No, you are not Lord Linwood here; I have degraded you; and you should not be even 'Master'. Immodest indeed!" Smacks, smacks, smacks on my cheeks. What could I do with my arms fixed?

"Am I immodest?" She smacked my face till I was silly. "You shall tell me when I have birched you."

As I lay under this perfumed girl, I really did not know how to contain myself. I experienced such sensations as I had never before had. There I lay on her bed on my back face uppermost, my arms fixed as if in a vice while she sprawled on the top of me her breath occasionally flaming my face harrowing my tenderest feelings and recollections mercilessly.

The idea of my bottom which was not safely hidden being exposed, and exposed to her! To her, a girl. Just think of all that she would see. Consider the shame. And consider her whipping it. The most shameful, most animal part of me flogged by a girl. What degradation. Here I should be, perfectly helpless, turned up like a baby writhing or not as she in her good pleasure chose. It was too humiliating. How should I ever again after such humiliation be able to hold up my head; how ever should I be able to look her in the face? I should have to perpetually hang my head. The idea she suggested of Laura whipping it was worse. The worse part of being whipped by a woman was clearly not the suffering; it was the power she thence derived over one by means of the exposure and of the pain she could inflict and the intimate relation in which it placed her. The abject condition in which it placed one under her. She could never again regard one as of any importance when she had made one twist and turn under the anguish of her lashes over whose bottom she could always brandish the rod. What man could hold his own with the woman who at any moment could say "I shall whip your bottom for you." It was indeed a terrible prospect; the sceptre, the birch, could not be defied. I trembled as I realized this. I tremble now at the recollection how amply my fears were realized. I resolved to resist to the uttermost. But every gesture of Mademoiselle sapped my powers. She spoke so freely, so recklessly, so archly, of what I could not think of without a blush, a girl and almost a stranger to me, she quite deprived me of my breath apart from the effect of the liberties she too, and her lolling upon me, which were of themselves more than sufficient to overwhelm a much less susceptible individual than myself. All possibility of establishing any bounds of delicacy vanished. I was helpless in her unscrupulous hands, she might, she no doubt would outrage me in a way that would be far worse than death.

"Yes" she continued, "Laura could not punish

you but I can. I shall delight in it, I shall punish you soundly as you have never been punished before.

"Your soul shall not be your own. I have no scruples. I shall make you feel, I shall torment you until you will grovel on the ground at my feet and beg and pray to be allowed to obey in order to be forgiven," and completely mistress of the situation she pushed me and pulled me and crushed me pinching my legs and slapping my face as she rolled on me. She constantly shifted her position in the course of her lecture and each time gave me fresh and overwhelming excitement.

I puffed and blew, I perspired, I was almost suffocated. To my horror she had several times hinted she would completely take off my trousers, several times her hand had played in an exasperating tantalizing fashion about my waist and the bracer buttons. At last she slipped it down and deliberately undid all the buttons of the flap. "Don't be shy" she exclaimed spreading the garment wide apart and pulling out the shirt, "let me see him." I panted, gasped, and shuddered almost dead with shame, and threw my head back. She rapidly uncovered my nakedness.

"What a state he is in," she laughingly said, playing with the engine of all my feelings. "Does that give you pleasure?" asked she, looking into my face as she pulled and twisted and squeezed the thing with her white hand. "Shall I lie on him?" grasping my shoulders and pressing her legs against me.

"Does that excite him more?" I dared not

speak, I was sick, exhausted with horror and despair.

"That is what you would have done with Laura, had you had your way" she remarked in anger regarding me with silence for a minute and then withdrawing her hand she gave me another severe and tingling blow with it on the face.

Finally to my utter consternation she announced her intention of then and there depriving me of my trousers.

"And of your drawers, socks, and shoes also" she added.

Excited and flushed, her lovely thick hair loosened by her exertions, she arose for the purpose.

"You shall write and tell Laura how I have avenged her by subjecting you to what you tried to make her undergo, you wicked abandoned young man," she remarked as again throwing herself on me. She held me down with her shoulder on the enormous pillow while her hands were busy around me with the buttons. The trousers, drawers, socks and shoes were very quickly unbuttoned, unfastened—too quickly—dragged off, and thrown upon the floor.

My shirt was violently turned up to my breast and there I lay in shameful nakedness before Mademoiselle d'Erébe, an extremely fashionable young lady and my governess, transfixed with the beauty of her back which was turned towards me and deprived of the covering necessary to conceal and protect my display of feelings.

Unable to help myself except by futile wriggling which only increased her amusement, I lay mad with vexation, nearly distraught with confusion, as she stood calmly contemplating me, kicking my legs about in a vain effort to hide my shame.

The thought at the moment of Laura nearly asphyxiated me. But this was not Laura. Such a plight before her could not have been without its consoling circumstances. She must have had compassion on me.

For the compassion of this damsel I did not care if even I could obtain it, my heart did not hunger for her; as yet she had excited such a storm of passion that it seemed very probably I should ere long be hopelessly involved in her toils, made her loving slave by a coup d'état.

But so far she was only my governess over whom I desired to maintain an ascendancy yet—here I was in this state, ready for punishment. Truly it was a terrible predicament. What regard could she ever have for me after having seen me thus? I tried to roll over. This she instantly prevented. What good after all would it have done? No doubt I should be made to roll over but too soon.

Her contemplation of my back, my bottom and my thighs would be even worse than her minute inspection of my front. I had particular horror of showing a young lady my bottom. It seemed to me that it would disgrace me as a man for ever.

The other thing she had as a young lady a certain specific right to see and handle and amuse herself with; it belonged par excellence to her sex, it was of no use except to them. But my bottom! I have long ago come to the conclusion that the cruellest part of the punishment by a woman is that she invariably whips the bottom and delights in it. It is so shameful, so ignominious, so utterly degrading, so absolutely humiliating. In that too she delights and glories. There are very few women who do not delight in the idea of whipping, the sense of complete power and the joy of acutely punishing the animal nature has an irresistible attraction to them. There are none who have once wielded a birch over a man who do not consider it the most exquisite pleasure they can have, one which they ever after perpetually love to enjoy. One essentially feminine.

When Mademoiselle had looked at and played with me as long as she cared to, she bid me turn over and lie on my face, I was not now however anxious to roll over and did not immediately obey; whereupon she snatched up the whip. I saw what was coming. In a paroxysm of fear I attempted to spring up. The attempt was nipped in the bud and rewarded with three or four slinging cuts across the fronts of my thighs delivered with such surprising good will that they made me howl.

There was no help for it.

Smothering my feelings as best I could, resigning myself to an inevitable fate in the shape of this inexorable damsel at the sound of whose voice and the mere rustle of whose petticoats (how in after years I have shuddered as I have heard the frou-frou of the same garments coming along the corridor to the room whither I had been sent to await whipping by the wearer) I had learnt to tremble.

There was no help for it. I turned over half crying, sobbing, she pulled my shirt up to my shoulders, examined and passed her hand over my bottom and legs even between them.

How I thrilled at each fresh touch of the cool soft hand!

Then she leant against my back and inserted her arm and hand right between my legs, well up, and through onto my abdomen. I spasmodically opened my legs wide. She rubbed me as a nurse would a child with a pain.

The sensations she gave me were intense. She knew it and observed that she would avenge Laura by flogging me soundly for my naughty feelings besides teaching me respect to herself in which she alleged I had been sadly deficient ever since I had come to the house.

How I wished I had never come there.

This torture over, she pulled a bench about nine feet long into the middle of the room, on it she placed a feather bolster. Along this urged by the riding whip she compelled me to lie down.

She fixed my ankles underneath together with leather straps tightly. The thick warm bolster between my legs caused a fresh wave of feeling I could not conceal and was deeply ashamed she should notice as she did. A short belt round the bench and the small of my back, and another round it and my neck completed the equipment and I was thus rendered absolutely helplessness.

She then opened a drawer and took out two long little elastic green supple birches well budded which she swished alternately through the air with vicious enjoyment and affectionate regard.

At each swish I cringed. I begged for mercy. I promised abject obedience, absolute repentance.

"You will obey?" she asked with a whisk of her petticoats.

"You will obey me?"

"Yes—Yes—Yes—Mademoiselle" swish, swish.

"You are sorry for your naughtiness?"

"Yes, yes."

"You will bring me your rifle, your gun, your fishing rods; will go out and come in only when I permit—will be in absolute subjection to me."

"Oh! Mademoiselle!"

"Will you?"

"Yes, yes."

"You will repent of your naughty feelings," catching hold of their organ as she again inserted her hand from behind and gave it a succession of terrible squeezes and pulls. "You will repent of them all—and come and tell me whenever you are troubled with them—eh? so that I may visit them with punishment?"

What a prospect! What could I reply? I felt the magnetic force of her petticoats, the prospective terror of the birch; "yes," I said reluctantly and desperately.

"Very well then, I shall only give you seven dozen."

"Seven dozen!" I uttered, aghast at such a fearful number.

But women have no idea of moderation in punishment, they love to exercise cruelty.

"Yes, seven dozen; or if you do not like the terms, twelve," she rejoined severely.

"Oh! only seven."

"You must ask me to birch your bare bottom; four dozen for Miss Laura, three on my account."

"Oh! oh!"

"And you must confess that you richly deserve them!"

I turned my head as much as possible, as much as the strap about my neck would permit. She was radiant with triumph there was a sparkle in her dark eyes sufficient to thrill the hardest heart. As she held up her robe with her left arm and with the beautifully formed right one flourished the spreading birch, she looked queenly-superb. It was not, I thought, such a bad thing to be under her, if I could, if free I would have poured out my soul and fervently assured her that for her sake I would have endured anything.

As it was I said "yes, Mademoiselle."

"Say what I told you."

"Please punish me!"

"That won't do—say after me, 'I have been guilty of the grossest attempt at indecence with Miss Laura and of the most persistent insubordination to you my governess. I promise to amend. And I ask you to birch my bare bottom most soundly and acknowledge that I richly deserve it'."

She stroked me as a cat plays with a mouse, caressingly as she uttered these words which with bated breath and shuddering frame, almost sobbing in dread of what would follow, I repeated after her.

"'And here after,'" she went on, "'I promise you on my honour the most abject submission, the most implicit and uncompromising obedience.'"

"Yes," I said.

"Say these words Charles," looking at me with such a glance as a tigress gives its prey before springing upon and devouring it. I repeated them.

"Seven dozen" said Mademoiselle with delight. "I shall flog you like a dog."

Coming closer to me, holding her robe still higher, giving her right arm full, strong the birch fell on my defenceless flesh eighteen times from left to right, eighteen times from right to left. I writhed, I twisted, I yelled. Such anguish from the arm of a girl I should have thought it impossible to experience.

She enjoyed it. Gloried in my agony.

"Now I shall punish that naughty thing," she laughingly said at the end of the third dozen, and standing at my head with the new birch gave me a dozen lengthwise.

The fact that she knew she was punishing it and did so deliberately increased my torment, my passions and my shame.

Now she rested. I twisted and sobbed and she calmly regarded me from an armchair.

She inserted her hand again and fingering me asked me if it repented its misdeeds or rather its naughty intentions.

I answered with a groan.

Taking the birch out of her hand into her right she gave me three dozen for herself, asking me between lashes whether I would obey, whether I would submit—abjectly.

I said I would I promised—I protested anything. She said she would presently test my obedience.

All of these last three dozen she gave me across remarking that "as yet"—ominous emphasis in these words—"it" had not offended her.

Then it was over: she left the room.

Returning in ten minutes she unstrapped me, and made me kneel at her feet between her knees, my arms still bound. I had to kiss her feet and her legs. She placed the soles of her feet one after the other on my mouth; she even gave me slight kicks; she said that next time she birched me she would put my head under her leg. This thrilled me. Then I was sent about my business. I was so sore I did not know what to do.

Half an hour later, I took my gun and a couple of dogs and went out. In the course of the afternoon I determined to set her at defiance, to write to my parents, never to allow under any consideration whatever a repetition of such treatment. I forgot my promise. I recollected and resolved to forget afternoon lessons. In quest of rabbits I travelled a long way through the park to a distant moor and farm house. Arriving there about tea time, Phyllis the daughter recognised me as the landlord's the Earl's son and gave me tea. She accompanied me on my homeward way. We reposed in the bracken. I could not confess to her that I had been whipped by the governess.

But as we lay there I put my arms round her and drew her on to me. One of her knees got between my legs and pressed me purposely. Excited I succeeded in getting a hand up her clothes, she blushed furiously and said I ought to be whipped, but she liked it.

Exactly what Laura had said, exactly what Mademoiselle had done.

This girl, this buxom country lass plucked a handful of bracken, and playfully lashed me with it. Seeing I enjoyed it she threw it away and rolled me on my back saying I was a proper young gentleman and placing her mouth on mine and leg across my legs, tore open my trousers in front and inserting her hand gave me such sensations as I had never before experienced not even from Mademoiselle.

She did not let me go until a crisis had occurred and then enquired whether that was better "than whipping my bottom" which at the same time she rubbed with her hand through my legs from the front.

I cringed but did not betray the cause.

I promised to meet her on a night she mentioned when she could be along and where she undertook to show me how a "lady" loved to be treated, and giving her a kiss and a couple of sovereigns, as it was getting late, I started for home.

Whether it was cowardly or not I had many qualms on my way home as to the reception I should meet with on my arrival. The nearer I drew to the house, the lower ebbed my courage what had become of my spirit, of the defiance which had inspired me but a brief time back in determination to rebel, and rebel successfully that I had no fear whatsoever. Why did I dread the mere idea of Mademoiselle's anger? A mere girl—had the petticoats already mastered me? What did I care for Mademoiselle; but at the same instant I recollected how she could flog—I would not however let her again catch me. I cringed notwithstanding, as I recollected how the excruciating agony of the chastisement she had inflicted, and how evidently she had enjoyed it. But to overcome it was necessary that I should encounter her. I marched on bravely. There must have been something enervating about my interview with Phyllis.

What a sweet lass she was.

What I wonder was it she had promised to teach me at our next interview—how delightful had been her treatment of me.

I lingered upon the soft memory of her embraces, her free and thrilling caresses unchecked as they had been by absurd notions of delicacy or anything of that sort, which so frequently interfere with one's enjoyment. False notions restraining one's mistress as well as one self from that which both long to do. What a misfortune it is that the most refined and charming women are usually those who are most subject to these nonsensical idiotic ideas.

To me perfect abandon is the greatest charm a woman can possess.

What an unconscionable time Phyllis had kept me. I had never for one moment intended being so late. I kennelled my dogs and entered by the back. I walked into the hall. The dining-room was silent. What a relief! Mademoiselle had forgotten all about me. Come? I would have some supper.

There were no men servants in the house so that in the hall I encountered a maid. She looked slyly at me with an intolerably quizzical expression that I saw at once meant—mischief and that made me most indignant. She informed me quite impudently that Miss Lisette wished to speak to me.

I felt still more uncomfortable but disguised the fact as best I could. Lisette was Mademoiselle's own particular maid.

A strong buxom country girl. I felt instinctively that I should be no match for her.

"Where are Mademoiselle and my Cousin?" I asked Ellen.

She answered they had gone out to dinner adding that Mademoiselle had been expecting me all the afternoon (whereat I smiled) and that she had left directions about me with Lisette who had desired to be informed the instant I came in. I felt my face grow long at this.

"All right Ellen, tell Lisette I am going to get some supper and she will find me in the dining-room if she wants to."

There was nothing to eat in the dining-room. The table and the sideboard were both clear.

What rubbish, I must have some food. These idiot girls. I angrily and violently rang the bell and in the meantime took out a bottle of Burgundy and filled a large glass as I felt a long drink was decidedly desirable at that juncture. Just as the bumper touched my lips Lisette walked in. She was smiling with a very complacent air. She had not had anything to do with me before and I believe was pleased that her turn had come at last. I offered her a glass of wine. It would be well to be on good terms with her. A little gallantry might win her over to my side. I held the bottle and was in the act of pouring out a second glass, having set down my own untasted for the purpose, when she calmly took the bottle out of my hands put in the cork and quietly saying:

"*Merci, M'sieur*" drank off what I had poured out for myself. She laughed in my face when she saw my anger and began hustling me about. I quickly lost my temper whereupon she followed suit and catching me by the collar bundled me off before her giving me violent thumps in the rear with her knees as she did so. She did not vouchsafe me any information whatever. When I proved refractory she gave me one or two sounding cuffs on the head much severer punishment than Mademoiselle's slaps. I soon found all attempts at resisting this virago useless.

I had not the necessary strength. She conducted me into Mademoiselle's bed-room and through it into a good sized closet opening off the bed-room. There was I noticed a firm wooden bedstead but no clothes on the bed which consisted only of a piece of stout rough canvas laced to the sides and ends of the wooden frame with cord.

At the head there was a bolster. There was no crockery in the room. The window was small and quite ten feet from the floor. The sash was shut or opened by means of a pulley and rope. Lisette showed me into this den so roughly that

I felt the tears rise in my eyes. She gave me no chance whatever of making friends with her. The impetus of her push made me fall across the seat, she went round it and drew up the window muttering something about my being a dirty little coquin, a miserable garçon, and inquiring how I dared set my governess at defiance, she caught hold of my arm and seating herself pulled me towards her, divesting me of my jacket, waistcoat and trousers before I knew where I was. Turning me round with a vigorous movement of her arm I speedily found myself face downwards across her lap, with my shirt over my head in front as well as behind receiving such a spanking from her massive hand as I had never imagined possible. The pain was fearful, her hand was so hard and heavy. She had got me well up between her legs and was plainly intended to obtain as much pleasure for herself as possible. She ceased, rested and began again, keeping me tightly down in the interval. I thought she would never stop. I knew I should be black and blue. I expected she would pound my flesh into a jelly. I was still very sore from the birching. I prayed for mercy. I cried and besought and protested and promised. All to no purpose, I could not escape. She told me if I did not take my punishment quietly she could only give me more and would not cease until I ceased yelping. Finally I cried quietly. At last she threw me exhausted on to the floor and gave me one or two kicks. Then she tore off my shirt and vest. She held up the first and examined it of course discovering the stains on the front from what Phyllis had done, and she said she could direct Mademoiselle's attention to it. She then strapped my hands behind my back, bundled up all my clothing under her arm told me I did not require any supper and left the room locking the door behind her and leaving me stark naked.

I felt too ill, too wretched to realise fully what a pretty fix I was in. Where were all my plans and schemes of enfranchisement, of rebellion now? Hour after hour passed. I called, I cried, I promised "Mademoiselle Lisette," "Barbara" only the echo answered. I became frantic. I could do no harm for my hands were firmly fixed or I do not know what I might not have done. I threw myself on to the seat, on to the bed, on to the floor. I felt cold. It rapidly became pitch dark. Would Mademoiselle return that night? Would she sleep in the next room? At length after the elapse of ages as it seemed to me she returned. She dazzled me with her beauty as flushed with enjoyment in light spirits and her very décolleté dinner-dress she appeared at the door.

"So you are my prisoner at last" she said, as holding a candle high up she gazed at me leisurely and voluptuously. "You seem ashamed at being found naked by me."

Well I might I thought as I regarded her exquisite swelling bosom all unveiled and her rounded white arm so well displayed by her attitude.

"I shall not allow you out of my sight again" she went on "and take care you do not get those handsome back settlements of yours again punished by Barbara and perhaps other young ladies also.

"That would put you to shame would not it? Where have you been all afternoon? We will postpone enquiry until the morning.

"But tell me now, have you made up your mind to obey and submit, or are you going to give me any more trouble?"

"I will try to be good Mademoiselle" I muttered, almost dead beat.

"That's right" seating herself. "Come and kneel at my feet kiss them; put my foot on your mouth"; through thin silk stockings I could feel the warm flesh.

"Kiss my ankles, kiss my hands, kiss my legs" she gave herself up to the sensual enjoyment my obedience provoked. I seized the opportunity gladly hoping to propitiate her. She once held my head for some minutes between her thighs as she lay back. She made me kiss her neck and her breasts. At length I was ordered to lie face downwards on the rough canvas of the bedstead. I feared more birching.

"No" she said "I shall not birch you now, I am going to fix you for the night."

Unstrapping my hands, she one by one fastened them to the posts at the head of the bed.

She similarly treated my feet. "I shall be back in a minute" she then said.

She returned with a large triangular hair cloth and all over the front long hogs bristles quite an inch in length stood out. It was in fact a large limp brush in the shape of a shield; she slipped it under me, the broad end across my breast. It pricked me cruelly. She smiled at my contortions and tied it across my shoulders. The apex of the triangle she inserted between my legs tight to my tenderest portions over my most sensitive organs and braced it up cruelly to the strap across my back. My weight drove the bristles in all over me.

"That shall be your wife for tonight" she remarked as, throwing a thick rug over me, she left me to sleep. Sleep! I was in agony. My torture I knew would however only serve to give her voluptuous sensations and lascivious ideas all night long.

"Your wife is to cure you of staining your shirt. Yes, Lisette showed me. I wish you happiness. I trust you will enjoy her embraces. Good night." and taking her candle, she left the room.

For the next weeks my liberty was grievously curtailed. Some days I got my way. Others Mademoiselle had hers. At last she said she would crush rebellion once for all.

And this brings me to the next chapter, but this account of one day at Holywell Hall gives a very good idea of the discipline I was constantly subjected to. It applies to many days and will show the subjection in which I was long kept.

Chapter III

Conquest

Here's a good world.
—Knew you of this fair work?
KING JOHN

It took quite a week for me to recover from the severe discipline of "my wife" and when that time was over and I felt better, as it was one of Mademoiselle's principles to punish periodically whatever my conduct, I had to undergo it again. Every week she married me as she facetiously described it, she even threatened to birch me in my wife's arms and only abstained for fear of really injuring me.

My interview with Phyllis never came off. Morning, noon and night I was never out of Mademoiselle's sight, or Lisette's, or Barbara's.

Once or twice I managed to escape for a few hours and Mademoiselle complained she had not yet succeeded in thoroughly subduing me, in thoroughly breaking me, in thoroughly conquering me.

She was determined to do so. One morning I was very refractory. And not without cause, I, a scholar, a young man, was set on a stool in the schoolroom where Mademoiselle, Barbara and two other young ladies were reading Dante, whom I understood much better than any of them, or than all of them put together, with a slate in my hands to do sums in simple addition. The girls giggled and laughed and poked fun at me at every opportunity until at last in a fit of indignation I threw my slate violently down on the floor, and declared I could not be made an ass of.

This was the crisis Mademoiselle had long been trying to bring about. It was a repetition of the first incident. She arose and slapped my face. I was obliged to protect it with my arms and hands.

"Your wickedness all arises from your masculine garments. I shall deprive you of them. I shall put you in petticoats."

How the girls tittered and how red they became.

"I shall subject you besides to the regime of the stay lace."

I did not know what she meant. She rang the bell.

Lisette was directed to bring a complete outfit of Barbara's and a birch. In the meantime Mademoiselle tied my hands with her own handkerchief, took down my trousers at my everlasting shame and made me stand in the corner. She asked whether one of her pupils could lend her an under petticoat and Beatrice, the most beautiful of the three, cried out.

"Oh yes I can spare one. I put on two flannel ones this morning as it was cold, but I find them too much, and shall be glad to get rid of one."

She slipped it off and Mademoiselle fastening it with the tapes at the waist made a bag of it which warm as it was and redolent of Beatrice, she slipped over my head and face. Then I stood with my trousers down to my heels, my shirt tails flapping about my naked legs awaiting Lisette's return, knowing that then my bottom would not only be exposed to the girls, but made to smart and burn for their amusement as I twisted and writhed and howled before them with a girl's flame red flannel petticoat over my head, face and shoulders.

Lisette came in, I trembled and began to sob. She roughly laid hold of me at a signal from Mademoiselle having deposited her armful of clothing on a chair.

I had been schooled into obedience and the thought of resistance did not suggest itself. Lisette took off, having unfastened my hands, my jacket and waistcoat, my trousers, socks and drawers besides of course the petticoat.

In nothing but my shirt Mademoiselle bid me come to her, where she sat looking like an insulted queen with the birch on her lap.

"Kneel down Charles, kiss the birch, now my hand."

Then she turned up my shirt out and pinned them across my shoulders.

"Now take the birch and go to Miss Beatrice—kneel down say. 'Please Miss Beatrice will you favour me by birching my bare bottom for being naughty. Please give me two dozen well laid on for that, and a third dozen lengthwise for the privilege of having been under your petticoat.'"

I sobbed out the humiliating words at Beatrice, a big girl of eighteen who was in a tremendous flutter of excitement almost choked by the violence of her feelings. I sobbed out the words, and Beatrice promised to birch my bottom well. There was a little tremor in her voice as she dwelt on these words, and let her eyes rest on my naked body.

"Now, Lisette," said Mademoiselle. Lisette caught me, led me to the ottoman and placed me across it face downwards. She pulled up my shirt higher and fully displayed my nakedness to the girls, at which I groaned afresh.

Then pressing her knee on my neck she told Beatrice to begin.

Slowly and leisurely with severe deliberation Beatrice gave me two dozen strokes, half from one side, half from the other and then, standing by Lisette, the third dozen lengthwise. I knew that if I did not take the punishment quietly I should only get worse. I stifled my sobs and cries; I could not help kicking my legs about.

When it was over I was told by Mademoiselle to stand up.

Beatrice resumed her seat looking satisfied and proud. I stood up trembling all over quite pale suffering agonies from the smart.

"Go to Miss Beatrice and thank her, say you will try to be good and not offend her again and ask permission to kiss the hand that punished you."

I complied with these humiliating directions.

"Now take the birch. Go to Lady Edith. Kneel down. Say 'Lady Edith will you please punish me for the disgraceful exhibition of myself which I have just made and for the insubordination to my mistress which rendered this discipline necessary by birching my bare bottom as much as your Ladyship may think proper. And as I have been very naughty please do not fail to lay the strokes on as severely as you can.'"

Now it was especially spiteful of Mademoiselle to make me say these last words, for Lady Edith was a strong girl of two or three and twenty, taller than any of us, a great horsewoman, a rower, a cricketer, and a very poor scholar. I knew she would take my request literally and comply with it with delight, I feared any hesitation about repeating the words would only betray my apprehension and direct more attention to them, so I said them as monotonously as I could, but Edith noticed and smiled, and immediately raised herself erect. I knew my bottom would be cut to ribbons. I had seen her punish a horse with spur and bridle and whip until the animal trembled and shook under her lathered with white foam from crest to crupper, every nerve quivering.

This Duke's daughter looked at me with great contempt as I knelt in my shirt at her knees. She drew herself up, more than once placing her hand upon her lips as she scanned me coldly. She was attired in a plain blue serge dress, the untrimmed body of which fitted closely over her admirable corset giving her a waist of extreme elegance and putting her well developed breasts well forward. She was so well drilled, her manner was so possessed and determined, that I anticipated I should derive more pleasure from receiving punishment from her although I knew it would be much more cruel than that inflicted by Beatrice.

I have seen it remarked in some book on this subject that it is the woman who is most severe, and most cruel, most inexorable, most merciless, who holds her pupil down most rigidly and whips him the most excruciatingly, who regards least or rather not at all his cries prayers protests and promises of amendement but relentlessly proceeds to inflict the full measure of the punishment, who gives most pleasure and who is most often requested to administer discipline; and this I know to be true.

There was a strange infatuation consequently, in requesting punishment from Lady Edith. I as ardently desired to receive the rod from her hands as J.-J. Rousseau from those of Mademoiselle de Pulson. She very soon found the state of my feelings, they required no confession, she divined them I know not how, and my condition gave her that pleasure which all women take in conquest by their own personal attributes. Lady Edith thought the better of me, for my susceptibility, but the glitter in her grey eyes told me that woman like she could take advantage of it to be all the more rigorous.

"Yes Charles," she replied with a gratified smile, looking full and boldly into my face and moving the lower part of her body lasciviously, "I shall have great pleasure in complying with your request. I am glad you have the sense to know you need punishment, for certainly your exhibition was a very indecent one to make to us ladies—and severe punishment I shall give you as you properly desire," stretching out her arm and looking at it, "I shall lay the strokes on as severely as I can, you may be sure of that, and considering your behaviour and boldness it would not be right of me to give you less than five dozen."

"Oh Lady Edith—five dozen!" I cried jumping up.

"Yes sir, five dozen," she answered, delighted to perceive that her mere sentence inspired me with terror beyond description. Lisette immediately seized me and was urging me to the place of execution but I struggled.

"Five dozen after all I have had of Miss Beatrice—oh Mademoiselle I shall faint, I shall die, I shall never survive."

"I shall not let you off Master Charles," said Lady Edith coldly, "you may depend upon it, that whipping is good for you" she continued as she stood up in her stately fashion, "and I shall whip you as soundly as I have ever whipped a boy."

It was notorious that she constantly and soundly flogged her younger brother whom she compelled to wait upon her. It was even said that the stable boys and pages had to attend in the morning in her apartment to receive the consequences of her displeasure.

The Duchess was dead, Lady Edith managed the establishment.

Mademoiselle said in answer to my appeal that I knew how to faint without hurting myself. Barbara and Beatrice simply delighted in my predicament. I burst into tears. Lisette caught me rudely and forced me on to the ottoman in position, my bottom well exposed, high up. I wriggled before my punishment began so much did I dread it. I felt before the first lash I should go mad. Was there no mercy to be found? Would not one of those pretty girlish forms show some mercy?

How hard it was that I a youth, a man, should be thus absolutely and abjectly in the hands of these women.

Where was the vaunted superiority of the male?

Lisette's knee pressed down upon the nape of my neck prevented any uttering a word. I shuddered as I heard Lady Edith walk over to me swishing the birch through the air. She walked with deliberate strides, showing none of the tremor Beatrice had manifested.

She stroked my bare flesh first with her hand, and next with the instrument of punishment, tickling me in a very agreeable tantalizing way. Then she stopped and stood a little way from me, I know, because her gown which had constantly rubbed against me while she was giving me the pleasurable sensations I have just described, ceased to do so.

I held my breath. Swish and the blow descended. The first three dozen were given with great precision and very scientifically from both sides well over the whole of my bottom which was so thoroughly warmed that it felt on fire. Lady Edith then asked for a fresh birch.

The last two dozen she divided into right strokes from one side right from the other, and right lengthwise and these last she gave along the legs and hips and not at all between them as Mademoiselle had done. The birch was very elastic, it had been well soaked and each of these twenty four strokes drew blood, my flesh was literally cut into ribbons. The sight of the blood rendered Lady Edith furious while the bleeding greatly relieved my anguish. Curious to relate, I really felt gratified to her for punishing me, I loved her for it, when I had recovered sufficiently I kissed her hand with fervour "I think you will remember me Master Charles, for a week or two."

"Yes I shall, Lady Edith," I sobbed.

It was impossible to punish my poor bottom anymore so Barbara and Mademoiselle gave me six cuts each with a riding whip across my thighs in front.

Lisette held me down on my back on the ottoman with my shirt right up to my throat, of course displaying my affair in front to the full and curious gaze of the young ladies who with many a sly jest and remark fixed their eyes upon it and noticed every movement.

This chastisement had the advantage of permitting me to see the lovely forms of my fair punishers and their graceful movements as the whip rose and descended with their arms. The pain was very hard to bear and the worse it was the more my tormentors smiled and enjoyed it.

At last it was over. It was Luncheon time. Lisette was directed to strip me naked and in that state I had to wait on the girls: when they had finished their cake and wine, Mademoiselle took me with her to the punishment closet opening off her room.

There she made me drink a quantity of red wine, and Lisette brought me soup and cake, rich plumcake, afterwards Lisette gave me a warm bath and Mademoiselle directed me to lie in her bed and sleep, she put on me one of her own diaphanous gossamer night robes bravely frilled and laced.

It was not a fresh one but one that she had worn the night before. How strange, but how happy I felt in the girl's bed. I had ceased somewhat to repent the loss of my freedom. The room was darkened and, exhausted, I slept.

At three o'clock Lisette brought me coffee and cream. She bathed my neck and face with cold water and having divested me of Mademoiselle's night gown took me naked back to the school room where were Mademoiselle, Barbara, Lady Edith and Beatrice.

A chemise of Barbara's was then thrown over my head.

Lisette next to my consternation and the delight of the girls, amongst whom there was a flutter of excitement, produced a corset. It was a Lady's, plainly.

My figure was not curved like that. It would never go into such a small space. I was least thirty inches round the waist and that horrid thing was not twenty two.

Lisette proceeded to adjust it.

Its bones were heavy and stiff.

It hurt me under the arms. I should be helpless in it, it was a strait waistcoat.

"Come Miss Charles you must have your stays put on."

"Oh Mademoiselle, they are ladies' stays—my figure is a male one; they will turn it into a female's."

"Exactly" said Mademoiselle, "you are to be turned into a girl."

"Not to be a boy any more."

"No more," decidedly responded Mademoiselle.

"But they hurt me, they press me so much, they are too small, I shall not be able to do anything in them," continued I, as Lisette on her part continued fixing the corset.

"They will teach you by the inconvenience to which they put you that you are not your own master, they will teach you the necessity of subjection to woman, their irksomeness will be a constant punishment of your impatience at her sway and their stiffness will enable you to appreciate the iron rule you are under. They are a lady's stays and that will constantly remind you that you suffer all this at her hands you will feel as if a lady were pressing you."

I blushed at the notion, so did the girls.

"Lace him to five and twenty inches" said Mademoiselle.

Lisette did so measuring me every now and then with a tape. At length my poor crushed waist measured but twenty five inches outside the corset I felt as if squeezed to death, unable to breath as though my ribs were fractured or driven into my lungs. I puffed and blew. The bust was so stiff I could not bend over. The stays were so long waisted that to prevent the curved bone being driven into me, I had to maintain a posture as erect as a grenadier's. As it was it hurt my male organ for which no provision had been made, very much when that gentleman attempted to raise himself. Mademoiselle and the girls enjoyed it all immensely. I felt the humiliation keenly. Mademoiselle walked up to me caught me by the bare arm turned me about and examined me, verified the correctness of Lisette's measurement herself, patted my bottom outside the chemise approvingly with her hand—the constriction above had made it swell out.

I mentally resolved to cut the lace at the first opportunity. My intention had no doubt been foreseen. Having examined me and displayed me for the girls—I cannot say how foolish I felt in Barbara's chemise with my bare arms neck and legs—Mademoiselle produced a metal chain silver or steel made of a number of broad plates to padlock and the place for the padlock could be inserted in its hole at spaces which were marked opposite each one. The largest was a girth of 27 inches; it went down to 16. Mademoiselle fixed the padlock at 25 and hung the pretty gilt key on to her watch chain where it tantalized me very much more than if she had put it into her pocket.

It was a pleasant summer's afternoon. The insects hummed lazily and contentedly about. The girls looked refreshed and bright. I should have liked to have been in a punt upon the lake under the green shade with Phyllis in close proximity, and as I had seen her already or some fresh but equally schooled wench. I do not care for your ingenue. I like the mistress who is so at once instinctively.

The air was balmy, soft and perfumed. Mademoiselle was never more ravishing. It was a stroke of art to clothe me in women's garments not in the morning but the afternoon. The poetry of the afternoon was more in unison. But as I looked eagerly through the open windows I longed for my trousers, my books, my dogs, my gun. This corset was a strait waist coat—how could I use a gun or leap a fence or pull a boat in it—the woman clasped me at the inception of each muscular movement and stifled it. It had an enervating effect on my whole spirit. There was something about it that sapped my virility.

I began to long my chains would embrace my conqueror and enjoy my abasement. Lisette interrupted my soliloquies by tumbling me back upon the ottoman and putting on me a pair of girl's long stockings, which came more than half way above my thigh. There was a difficulty about the suspenders which mademoiselle would not allow to be underneath the corset. I had never had girl's stockings on before, and I think they suggested effeminacy to me quite as much and as forcibly as anything else, even the drawers which came next and were a great trial. I blushed. Mademoiselle blushed. Barbara, Edith and Beatrice were overwhelmed. Lisette blushed but retained her *savoir-faire*. They were put on and then the petticoats. Short ones only just below my knee too. I cannot possibly imagine any word or expression which would adequately convey how indecent I felt; and as soon as I began to feel immoral that curved steel stay busk hurt me terribly.

At tea time I was baptised. Charles no longer. There occurred a protracted discussion as to what my name should be.

"Carola" suggested by Beatrice, Mademoiselle dismissed it as too masculine. Barbara suggested "Henriette" but it was deemed too stately. "Agnes," "Mabel," "Lilian," "Isabel," "Maud," "Sophia," "Clothilde," "Julia," "Anne,"

"Caroline," "Eleanor," were one by one dis-
cussed.

"What pretty legs she's got" said Beatrice,
"could she not be named 'Legulla' or 'Jambon'
or 'Gigot,' or something of that sort?"

"Call her 'Jenny,'" said Lady Edith, "it will
make her feel nondescript."

The proposal was received with acclamation
and "Jenny" I was dubbed; there was no dignity
about the appellation and it was ignominiously
feminine. In my short frock and striped starred
petticoat which kept my garments away from
my person I felt extremely sensitive, Beatrice's
reference to my legs covered me with confusion
and again I found the bowed busk underneath
my belly hurt me horribly. I resolved to have no
more sensations.

Alas my resolution was very short-lived.
Mademoiselle noticed that I kept hugging my
skirts down. She said a little shame would be
wholesome for me. Lisette was sent for. She was
told to take off my frock and petticoats and run
a tuck of six inches deep in them. I was
abandoned in the mean time in my drawers and
corset to the sport of Mademoiselle and the
three girls, what sport they made of me what a
ridiculous figure I was. I longed then if I ever
did for petticoats.

When they were brought back and put on I
could however have much sooner been without
them; they came down to within but three
inches of my knees; and made my nakedness
visible and remarkable. Especially when
Mademoiselle exasperated by my consequent
awkwardness and instigated by a spiteful

suggestion of Beatrice's allowed that damsel to deprive me of my drawers. However I could sit my bare legs from the tops of my stocking were then plainly to be seen. I felt quite overcome as I felt Beatrice's arms about me removing the linen things. Mademoiselle then thought that I really must be very tired after all I had gone through and told me to lie on the sofa.

Of course I had to obey very reluctantly.

"Clasp your hands behind your head, Jenny, let us see your pretty arms."

"Don't be embarrassed my dear" said Lady Edith, "be quite at your ease, draw up your left leg and rest your right foot against its knee." I assure you the posture had much to recommend it the couch, faced with large window between which and me they were all seated.

Reckless and frantic I assumed the desired position, and of course displayed all I had got.

Barbara wanted to know what that great thing that kept wagging in front of me, and remarked that no other girl had it.

Mademoiselle took a blue ribbon three yards long and tied it round it, giving me several sharp blows with her knuckles as she did so, the ends of the ribbon she then fixed to her own wrist and while they amused themselves she gave me more jerks than one. I to my surprise found a delight in this captivity.

The next morning when I was dressed a steel triangular purse was fastened to the ends of my corset in front. It was drawn over my male engine; the only male thing I had left, and through between my legs and was padlocked behind.

It was only removed for certain purposes after breakfast, after lunch, and before going to bed. I had to ask each time before the girls, or manage as best I could without having it unlocked.

With this safeguard of which Mademoiselle alone had a key, I was frequently left along with Barbara and the rest. They hustled me, lay upon me, fingered me, took all kinds of liberties with me.

And Mademoiselle turned me into her maid, I had to brush her dresses, clean her boots, put them on. Many a blow, a wrinkle in her stockings has cost me.

The riding habit was above all a trial. She used her spur severely upon her horse and the garment was stained with the animal's blood. Brush, wash, rub as I could I could not get them out.

"There is my habit in a disgraceful state again Jenny" said Mademoiselle in her trousers "how can you expect me to put it on like that, you careless good for nothing slut.

"Lie across the bed," flourishing her riding whip, "I will teach you to do your work more carefully."

"Oh Mademoiselle, I have tried and tried and they won't come out."

"No excuses, Miss! do not add lies to your idleness. Across the bed at once."

Lash, lash, lash, yell, yell, yell.

"Six more for lying" lash lash lash.

"Now come with me," and she led me to the coal cellar and locked me in, and left me there, with the rats and mice and blackbeetles for the three or four hours she was out. When she came home to tea or dinner or whatever it might be I got none till the habit was cleaned.

At last she discovered the habit was indelibly stained and then, vexed, she flogged me for not having told her before.

I gave up in despair. I submitted completely, abjectly, I lived in submission, a slave absolutely to Mademoiselle.

At last I began to hug my chains. But I was thoroughly conquered and had for months to enjoy the woe of the vanquished.

Chapter IV

Vae Victis

Falling and brawling, and sprawling
And driving, and riving, and striving.
SOUTHEY

"Go to my bedroom, Jenny, at once" said Mademoiselle one fine morning to me at breakfast. I was very hungry and had not begun, "and fetch my po, just as it is, mind."

I went and returned with the article in which was some of the clear limpid fluid from Mademoiselle's own person. Beatrice was staying in the house at the time. She and Barbara were in the room. As usual I was in a very short frock and a tightly laced corset.

"Take it to the closet and empty it, then bring it back and you are not to rinse it." I did so.

"Now take your napkin—wipe it out—bring it here—then there is your porridge milk and sugar" said Mademoiselle putting them into the po—"you are to eat out of it and when you have done you shall have your tea in it with your bread and butter—sit down there on the floor and begin or I shall birch you until you do."

My feelings of disgust and nausea were intolerable.

"I shall exact abject submission," said Mademoiselle, "I shall make you put your head in the po, and—and—do something in you, if you hesitate—you must submit to your mistress."

"Oh Mademoiselle, anything."

"No, no! not anything, no nonsense; obey."

I thought I should vomit the food. I wished I

had wiped the utensil drier, I had had no idea of the use my governess intended to put it to.

I ate the porridge out of the po, to Barbara's and Beatrice's huge satisfaction. They considered it a very suitable and proper punishment.

Then my tea was poured into it, drinking out of the vessel, which entailed touching it with my lips was worse than eating out of it.

At Lunch I had to get it and my lunch was put into it. The same at tea and dinner. After each time I had to replace it.

Mademoiselle used it in the ordinary way; all the week this discipline continued.

I got however so cantankerous about it that one day after luncheon she took me to her room and stripped me, put me into a bath with a strap across my chest. It was a long narrow bath tilted up at the foot.

She stood across me lifted her skirts to her waist displaying her shapely legs. Quite unconcernedly she then opened her drawers. I saw something hairy. She gazed at me. I looked at it. It moved. A copious stream suddenly fell on my ears, my mouth, my eyes, tingling, smarting, burning, she was peaing on me. I opened my mouth to cry out—down went the hot fluid and before I could save myself, it got to the back of my throat and would have choked me if I had not swallowed it. Mademoiselle laughed, the moment I opened my mouth she directed the volley there. I must have swallowed a pint of it. In the course of the lessons, Beatrice provoked me, and I made a hasty rejoinder.

Beatrice by Mademoiselle's orders smacked my face. The bath was sent for. I was once again stripped, strapped down and Beatrice told to pea on me and she did so. I was left strapped down during the lesson time.

Presently Lady Edith begged to know whether she might use the same convenience. Mademoiselle assented.

Barbara followed. I was unfastened then or I should have been drowned in urine.

My fishing rods, my guns, my sticks were brought to Mademoiselle by Lisette and Ellen.

Mademoiselle said a young lady had no use for such things. She broke the beautiful delicate rods across her knee and striking me with the fragments ordered them to be used for firewood. The guns she had packed and sold to a second hand dealer who was written to and who came for them. I was then made to sit and sew. She and the girls frequently went out and usually left me at home.

On these occasions I was dressed in a sleeveless bodice; long, very tight Suede gloves, twelve buttons each, were put on my hands and arms. A thread was wound round the buttons and sealed with a little gold seal Mademoiselle always wore at her chain, bearing her coat of arms in a lozenge.

Any attempt to remove the gloves would have been at once disclosed by the thread which could not have been replaced.

The gloves were generally white.

The object was to keep me good and quite out of mischief. When Mademoiselle came home she took an early opportunity of examining the gloves which of course showed the slightest stain. At first I was rather careless, amused myself, moved chairs, opened doors, ran about as usual, and used my hands as I found occasion to without thinking of the consequences. I did not do so however a second time.

As soon as Mademoiselle had returned she sent for me to her boudoir. Whip in hand she scrutinised the right arm and hand, and then the left arm and hand. They were both very dirty; she said so. I explained that I could not help it; she smiled and holding my right hand by the wrists cut it eighteen times with the whip.

The tight glove made the pain excruciating. I begged, I prayed, I implored mercy, she merely smiled and observed that another time I should she supposed somehow manage not to soil my gloves, they were ladies' gloves. Then she treated the left hand in the same way.

I danced and writhed and wrung my hands.

She gave me some severe and stinging cuts about the legs because of the noise I made, to finish up with. On the next occasion I was sitting with my hands folded not daring to use them for anything, when Lisette whose order I had to obey during Mademoiselle's absence come to me and said she had upset a box of pins and beads in the work room on the floor, and wished me to pick them up. I am convinced Lisette upset them purposely.

I protested and explained that I dared not soil my gloves for anything she could give me.

"I will give your bottom a rare good birching

Miss Jenny if you do not do what I tell you."

"Oh Lisette, how unkind! you know what trouble you will get me into."

Lisette only smiled.

"Perhaps" she said, "if you were not so disagreeable about pleasing me I should me more merciful."

I knew what she meant.

Lisette had had me in the workroom one warm afternoon and she I suppose felt very naughty. At any rate she wished to put my head under her clothes and made me kiss and lick her. She knew about the peaing on me and said I had seen what she required me to kiss to give her pleasure. I dared not tell. Mademoiselle Lisette had got my hands tied behind me and was pushing me down. She had already raised a stalwart leg to put it across my shoulder and had got my head against the other one, I was almost caught when she got called away.

"Will you be more obliging today Miss Jenny?"

A strange thrill came over me. Often while lying awake too I thought of what Lisette wished, and that it could not be so very disagreeable after all. The idea made me feel very naughty, to have my head between a maid's legs unable to get up until she permitted, being made to kiss and lick her most sensitive and secret parts.

"Would you like me very much Lisette?" I asked mischievously.

"Come and you shall see!" I went to the workroom. She shut the door and sat down putting her legs well apart and slightly drawing up her skirts. There were the pins and beads, a heap of them all over the dusty floor. If I had to pick them up my gloves would be dreadfully soiled and when Mademoiselle returned I knew my hands would tingle for the next six hours in consequence.

"Come here" she said and putting her hands on my shoulders pressed me down.

"Sit in front of me on the floor."

She soon forced me down and lifted her leg— the sight of her common underclothing and the strong scent were too much for me. She had not fastened my hands this time I sprang up under the uncontrollable impulse of a strong revulsion of feeling.

"I won't, I won't!" I shouted.

"You wretch!" she exclaimed, fiery red, her amour-propre offended and hurt, "you wretch!" She hit my face and head four, five, six times with her hard hands. She forced me on to the couch and soon got my face under her clothes between her legs, she pressed my mouth and rubbed herself against me. It was sickening. Presently my face was covered, I could not open my mouth, with a sticky warm fluid my eyes and nostrils were saturated with it. Then she seemed satisfied.

Next she ordered me to pick up the pins and beads threatening to cut me with the whip.

Utterly overcome I set to work. She would not wash my face.

It took me quite an hour and a half. I at last carried her the box.

"Kneel down and hand it to me, you little pig."

I did so.

She upset it on the floor again and I had to pick them all up a second time.

My gloves were in a fine state. I was wild with terror. When I took the box the second time to her, she set it down, got up, and upset the coal scuttle. She forced me to replace the coals with my fingers.

When Mademoiselle returned that night she was furious.

She fixed my hands and arms to the back of two chairs and lashed them until she was tired. I yelled and screamed. She said I had deliberately defied her.

She then condemned me to two and a half inches tightening of my corset for six hours which almost suffocated me.

She next took me to the punishment room threw me on my face on the bed, fixed my feet soles uppermost to its foot and lashed them with the riding whip.

Of course I required no dinner that night. I was kept in that room until she went to bed when six hours had elapsed.

The details of the backboard, the stocks, the drills, all handy instruments of punishment which Mademoiselle knew well how to use, I must leave to the reader's imagination.

I will only mention one diabolical invention. Buttoned up in a jacket into the sleeves of which steels had been sewn so that I could not bend my arms or put my hands near my head, she would fix silk strings into my hair at the back and fasten them to the top of my corset keeping my chin consequently high in the air I have had to endure all day long sometimes and the torture the ache the pain in my neck are indescribable.

Chapter V

The Secret Source of the Power

Infus et in jecote ægro
Nascuntus domini.
PERS. SAT.

Our passions play tyrants in our breasts. What was there about these petticoats so alluring, so enervating, so emasculating? Why, when I had to clean my governess's gloves, polish her boots, brush her dresses, was there something thrilling about the work? Why did the garments electrify me, why did I revel in my bondage, grovel in my subjection, hug my chains, think of my tormentor with hatred breath and a secret affection? Of Barbara I had became fond and many were the stolen caresses and endearments we enjoyed.

But with Mademoiselle, I was in love. It is not too much to say that I sometimes sought punishment because of the pleasure I had in receiving it at her hands. She found this out and make good use of the weapon to reduce me to still further subjection.

I enjoyed being about her I loved sleeping in the room next to her. I kissed her pretty ankles with fervour when I took off her stockings. I asked as a reward to be shut up amongst her skirts in her wardrobe. To such an extent did I love her flesh and all that had contact with it.

My schooling had been going on for many months now, and I had quite forgotten I had ever been a boy.

I noticed Mademoiselle's delight in punishing me, and wondered how and why it could give her pleasure.

I had made up my mind to obey unhesitatingly her least wish, to anticipate her desires, and she soon found out the alteration. She in consequence permitted me to make love to her, to express my motive to assert my love. One afternoon a half holiday, instead of going out I asked permission to remain indoors. I knew she was going to stay in her boudoir and I hoped to be allowed to pass the time in her company in which as I have explained, notwithstanding all her hard usage of me, owing to some infatuation I took a strange but very real delight. Mademoiselle looked at me curiously and assented. Her boudoir was a charming room full of quaint old furniture, old china very cosy and luxurious. It was upholstered in blue which set off her dark beauty admirably and there were bowls of roses about filling it with a delicious intoxicating perfume. Mademoiselle always wore a large bouquet of flowers in her corsage, roses were her favourites. She invariably wore them when she had any one to whip. I have noticed a passion for perfume and the birch usually go hand in hand. Dressed in an elegant tea gown, she lolled in a great chair looking ravishingly lovely, her soft figure showing to perfection, and made me kneel some distance away from her on the floor. An hour passed thus while she read and took no notice of me. At last she closed her book looking a little bored.

"Well Jenny, would not you much rather be out with the others than kneeling there gazing at me. What are you thinking about?"

"Of you, Mademoiselle" I replied blushing.

"Of me" she rejoined archly with a pretty affectation of surprise "of me, are you thinking of fainting?"

"Oh Mademoiselle" I ejaculated confused.

"There is a couch" pointing to a large divan in which were some big pillows "all ready, you must be tired of kneeling so long—suppose you lie down upon it—perhaps I may kiss you if you don't faint—if you do I shall be angry and—and—in that case should probably b-i-r-c-h you," she said, dwelling upon the word, her eyes flashing as she pronounced it: and a flame still remaining in them as she mored.

"Oh Mademoiselle, I do not know which I should like best!"

"What! kissing or birching?"

"Yes," I said as red as a peony, "from you."

"You strange creature; you enjoy your subjection then: you like me to punish you."

"Yes!"

"Why, I wonder" delighted and coming over to me as I rolled on the couch. "What is there that can be nice about it—it must hurt horribly?"

"It does, but it is from you; and to you it is entrancing to be subject."

Now this was indeed a question with which I had over and over again puzzled myself. Why indeed was it delicious to be ordered about by Mademoiselle. It was not because she was Mademoiselle Diane d'Erébe, but simply because she was Mademoiselle. I felt there was some secret which I had not unearthed. No tutor for instance could have affected me in that manner as she did; as she did.

Did the mystery lie in her petticoats? She had a softer skin, more voluptuous form, more rounded limbs than a man. But she had two legs, two arms. Petticoats were extraneous, what however did they express? True, she had two deliciously soft luscious breasts, and no hair on her face, while men have rank faces and a mere mockery of breasts. Their teats merely put on satirically—it always has seemed to me.

"And why to me?" she repeated mischievously, an amused smile playing about the corners of her mouth. The mystery was one I could not readily fathom but I felt her influence upon me was far from being imaginary as I lay back beneath her gaze on the couch and she bent her elegant form across me, giving a sense of restraint by her proximity which was extraordinarily sweet.

"I fear" she continued, "you are too susceptible to the influence of the other sex. It is an instinct, a psychological enigma for which you cannot account, eh?" seating herself beside me and gazing into my eyes. "I will attempt a practical explanation," putting her left arm, across my large breast and leaning upon me.

At that instant a delicious confusion at my feminine attire and at its shortness overcome me, my long legs were scarcely covered to the knee by my frock and petticoats, increased my sense of helplessness in the hands of this charming girl.

"I am mistress of that which is master of your body and soul—you shall see if I am not—and the visible symbol of my sway is the petticoat. I shall now tame you completely, and prove to your satisfaction, prove conclusively, undeniably, how irresistible my feminine rule is."

She lay closer to me and stretched out her right arm so as to slip the sleeve away from the wrist and then promptly with a suddenness which took my breath away inserted it under my garments and going straight to the mark firmly grasped that organ which was the seat of my sensations, with her cool soft hand.

I gasped and wriggled and exclaimed but she would not let it go.

"No you shall not attempt to conceal your feelings from me. You are in my hands literally and I shall make you do what I please."

She increased the intensity of my emotions by carelessly throwing a leg across me.

I hugged her, I tried to kiss her face, I could only succeed in kissing the dress about her waist.

She held me very tightly and looked into my eyes but said nothing as she continued squeezing me vigorously.

I felt as though I was gradually absorbing her being. I felt she was ravishing my senses and myself of all control of them and over my mind whatever she bid me to do I felt I should be compelled to execute.

I implored a cessation as I knew something dreadful would otherwise occur though what I did not know.

She only laughed and redoubled her efforts.

My legs were wide apart and I gave myself up to the strange passions which she excited and by which she mastered me.

I remembered what Phyllis had done and

what had happened. Whatever should I do, if the same thing took place with Mademoiselle? I should be disgraced and never be able to hold my own with her even to the small extent to which up to that time I had managed to hold it.

"Shall I send for Beatrice" asked Madeoiselle, "or Barbara or better still Lady Edith?"

I am sure she asked to tease me.

"And let them witness your subjection?"

"Oh no, no, please, not on my account."

Her hand ruthlessly continued to work. Amongst the other emotions excited by it was an intense longing to come into close intimate contact with her, I made several attempts to touch her, to insert my hands under her skirts but quite uselessly. I was altogether beside myself and incapable of any real effort.

And then she began talking to me about ladies and their bright eyes and forms and questioning me about my ideas of their love, a subject and an examination which in that position thrilled me through and through. I felt the supreme moment could not be much longer postponed and that she would shortly receive an absolutely sincere confession—in her hands of my sentiments.

She asked me whether I knew what ladies were like, what they had under their petticoats "between their legs up here you know" squeeze squeeze "do you think they have a thing like this?" giving it an extra tug to denote what she meant.

"Yes — I — oh — oh — oh — I suppose so — oh, Mademoiselle."

"You ridiculous boy, do you mean to say you

do not know?"

"No I don't."

"Come, no fibs. Laura told me you touched her."

"I only felt something hairy."

"You wicked wretch!" ejaculated Mademoiselle, moving voluptuously, "well I shall make you feel and see and taste."

"Oh—oh—how?"

"You tried to put your hand under Laura's petticoats. I shall put your head under mine and increase your knowledge of anatomy."

"Between your legs — your legs, Mademoiselle?"

"Yes, between my legs, between my bare legs and keep you there until you have kissed and fondled and—and—satisfied me."

However the idea was too much. The passion with which she vibrated was contagious and soon communicated to me, my veins seemed in fire. I could restrain myself no longer and with a deep sigh—a gasp—the delicious convulsion overtook me—throb—throb she did not withdraw her hand; its continued pressure gave me delightful although real torture, as she pressed her ruby lips upon mine I became, I felt, utterly indifferent to all the women in the world but her.

The mechanical ebullition of feeling was however succeeded by a sense of disgust and degradation in which I suppose my spiritual nature recoiled upon the animal.

To this however especially as I was in a transport or kind of dream I did not pay particular attention.

What occupied me, was the task of comparing what Mademoiselle had done to me and the effect she had produced with my recollection of what Phyllis had done in the wood. Was this what all women did? Was it the beginning and end of all they could do to a man? Then I vaguely remembered Lisette. But I regarded her as a monster. And in the next place I indistinctly called to mind having made acquaintance with Phyllis's plump legs. I did not take any particular notice of what more I touched, I remembered only that it was a soft wet warm and very hairy thing; what its form might be I had no idea. Mademoiselle had excited my curiosity. I now resolved to avail myself to the uttermost of the opportunity of examining feminine anatomy which I was promised and the resolution excited my lust.

Without much hesitation, then, I obeyed Mademoiselle when she sat down in, it seemed to me, a strange although mild ecstasy in a low arm chair and, stretching her legs wide apart (indecently I thought), bade me sit on the floor between them. That done, she whisked her skirts over my head and slipping forward in the chair soon clasped my head very firmly with her bare thighs, for I found she had not drawers on. In front of me I felt (I could not see) a wet hairy protuberance. This was persistently pressed and rubbed against my mouth and a series of vicious kicks administered to my back by Mademoiselle's little heel, which hung at my waist behind, her leg being across my shoulder. Presently I found amidst the hair what seemed to be a mouth set lengthwise. It possessed a marvellous power of distension and soon enveloped my mouth and even my nostrils.

The kicks continued and became more severe. They began to hurt. I was sore from them and tried to move in order to protest. The scent besides was very powerful and I did not altogether appreciate my face being smeared with the sticky fluid which abounded in that locality; but a prompt grasp of the warm round legs held me fast.

I opened my mouth; the kicks ceased but the movements of the centre of Mademoiselle's body increased, another kick and I inserted my tongue, I took it out again immediately on receiving a blow on the back; I then pressed what was required of me and with a groan again opened my mouth and glued it with fierce resignation to the aperture. I kissed her, I bit her, I licked her, a strange fury or enthusiasm took possession of me. She threw her legs wide and lay back in her chair I caught her legs with my arms and pressed my face against her. At length she seemed to abandon herself to her sensations, there was a moment's lull, a little cry, and she was overtaken by the same sort of paroxysm I had suffered, my mouth was filled, my face covered by the inundation of what she ejected in spasmodic throbs. At that instant I was absolutely dominated by the feminine idea, by the female, by the sex, by Mademoiselle in particular. That domination I have never been able to throw off.

I never shall be able to rid myself of it.

Never, I fear!

I cannot see underclothing now in a milliner's

shop, women's underclothing, without a sense of the influence.

Pretty ankles and the frill of a petticoat carry me out of myself.

The mere frou-frou of a Lady's garments entirely deprives me of all self-control.

Mademoiselle still held me under her legs. I kissed them I hugged them. She allowed me to move my head down to her knees but not to rise.

So some ten minutes passed and I heard her and turning over the leaves of a book. She was reading. She would not however permit me to rise.

Presently I heard a slight exclamation and her heel was again firmly pressed against my back. This time I knew what to do.

I did it. It required more effort and a longer effort. At length the same thing happened but not so violently.

Again I hoped to escape from my confinement. The hope proved vain. Those relentless legs held me tight.

I had time to relish the position to dwell upon its sweetness to consider it in all its aspects. Then under a young lady's petticoats I had the most extraordinary feelings and ideas.

About an hour elapsed and a third time I had to perform, I was tired and went to work reluctantly.

"If you don't do it properly, Jenny" said Mademoiselle, lifting her garments for the purpose, "I shall birch you—birch you until you bleed. I shall flog you." How fiercely she spoke.

At last it was accomplished.

I loved Mademoiselle and my love was based upon the intimate knowledge of her carnally and spiritually to which I had been admitted— but there remained a strange longing to be more intimately united. There had been no union although close contact.

After the third spasm of physical rapture which my governess compelled me to cause her she reclined for some ten minutes or more in her chair as though fatigued and exhausted and possessed besides by same dreams of delightful nature to which she abandoned herself. Her legs were wide apart but her feet were crossed behind my back and not even yet allowing me to rise she permitted me to rest my head against her knees, I was not without certain sensations of my own.

It struck me at the time and I afterwards learnt it was the fact that a man in order to possess power must to a certain point be immoral. He cannot otherwise please the ladies. It surprised me much to find also what complicated machines women are. Many for instance whose physiognomy has shown me plainly that they were voluptuous and sensual, could in the most ingenious and seemingly absolutely sincere manner repudiate all knowledge of pleasure and all delight in it. While the demurer ones full of modesty and shame I found could never for a moment resist an indecent suggestion.

Women are terribly afraid of being found out in anything which is generally thought not respectable, they fear to lose caste, this exercises the greatest restraint upon them and leads them to heroic self denial—but woe betide the man who cares for such matters—upon his head they pour the fury of their contempt and regard him with bitter hatred as a milk sop or nincompoop. These women need encouraging to set respectability at defiance. They are too weak to do it alone and intensely grateful to him who induces them to do it.

The other class delights in the exercise of the feeling of shame.

A girl of this sort never gets over the pruriency caused by her being made to, for instance, take off her drawers before even her governess alone, or by her being whipped, that is having her bottom whipped by her tutor.

This reflection suggested Mademoiselle's recent threat of birching my bottom, and again the idea of a young lady having it exposed to her overwhelmed me especially while I was a close prisoner under that lady's legs and so near to the fountain of her womanhood.

I felt that organ with which she had played growing inconveniently, accompanied by a strong glow of my troublesome feelings. I felt that organ I had kissed triumphantly developed.

The idea struck me as though it were an inspiration. It was perfectly novel to me; suppose I could put that long thing between those delicious lips of flesh I had been kissing; suppose I could get it right in and that it grew in there until penetrated into the most intimate and secret recess of the woman; suppose that instead of pushing herself against my mouth and tongue the sweet combat were transferred to that male engine already fiercely rampant at the mere notion; suppose that the delirious impulse was continued until the spasm which we had separately experienced overtook us simultaneously! Would it not be exquisite; how delicious to sink into the embrace, into the soft limbs, into the body of her who would then become the dearest in existence, how entrancing to become reciprocally conscious of the sweetly shameful operations of each other's most secret parts. What woman could I induce to allow me to do so with her? Would Mademoiselle? I looked at the ivory white legs before my eyes, whose warm pressure I felt about my face and at the sphinx-like entrance between them to Mademoiselle's body upon whose lips there appeared to be an mysterious smile. She moved and an electric thrill went through me. She had magnetised me, mesmerised me.

I was no longer master of myself but governed by her lightest movement.

"Get up" said Mademoiselle, presently pulling herself together with a merry smile upon her rosy face. "Get up and . . ." taking out her dainty handkerchief, "let me tie this about your face that you may lose none of the aroma."

She tied it about my face and gave me a playful but smart slap. "What did you do with what I gave you?"

It must be owned that I had spat out as much as I could of it. Mademoiselle soon discovered this from the state of my neck and body and also of my handkerchief which she made me display to her.

"How dare you treat the choicest marks of a

lady's favour in that way?" she asked angrily, and seeing me confused, added: "You should have swallowed it all eagerly."

I swallowed some—I had been compelled to. The favour was still in my mouth; doubtless the relish of it is an acquired task as I did not then at all like it.

"Some, you insolent minx. Very well, I shall punish you. I know how to, come with me to my dressing-room directly, you shall swallow something much less agreeable!"

She caught me by the arm and led me there.

"Undress—quick—lie down in that bath so."

She strapped me across the chest lifted her petticoats and peaed in my face. I had to swallow quite a pint of the hot yellow beastly fluid.

"Now," she said, "you shall lie naked in my bed and as you have so behaved when I permitted you to kiss me in front, why then you shall be compelled to kiss and insert your tongue—behind—yes behind."

"Oh Mademoiselle, I cannot, I—I—I—won't," exclaimed I, horror stricken and disgusted beyond measure at the prospect. Nothing should induce me to do it.

"Then," said Mademoiselle with cold deter-mination, "you shall be birched until you do."

What with her urine down my throat filling me with horror of myself and the horrid performance I as now regarded it I had been made to go through, and what with the prospect before me from which I knew there could be no escape, I burst into tears which further exasperated Mademoiselle so that she tied me up in my bed-room, locked the door and left me there while she went down to the drawing-room to tea.

"Think about it, Jenny" were her last words. "Behind you know, I wonder how you will enjoy that!"

A greater degradation was in store for me before the night.

In about three quarters of an hour, Mademoiselle returned and not alone. She opened the door of communication between her own and my room and displayed me bound and naked to her companion, a tall strong magnificent woman of quite fifty. I had never before seen such an animal or a woman, she had such a passion in her eyes. She terrified me, such a tiger like aspect in such an elephantine feminine form.

She gazed at me fiercely for several minutes as though she would devour me, scanning my delicate frame, my white boyish form from head to foot like a cannibal; as though indeed she were about to butcher me—in fact she went as near doing so as she could. Without depriving me of life, she deprived me of all else, of all self-respect, of all desire of existence. She made me base, contemptible, hateful in my own eyes. It was a terrible and cruel punishment to subject me to on the part of Mademoiselle.

The advent of this lady was no doubt an accident and Mademoiselle determined to make use of it to revenge herself upon me for the slight signs of disgust I had displayed.

If I had thirsted for and swallowed what she had given me this I felt would not have occurred.

"Well Mademoiselle" said this person at the conclusion of her leisurely inspection "so you have a very obstreperous youth in your charge."

"Yes, Lady Digwell, you may well say that."

"I see you have subjected him to the regime of the stay lace and discipline of lady's drawers and petticoats,'" she continued, glancing at my clothes which lay in a confused heap as I had thrown them on my bed, and taking up the corset, "that is right."

"It does not seem to have done him much good."

"Oh never mind, dear Mademoiselle, I think I can promise you to cure him and improve him, he only needs a little corrupting.

"Corrupting, Lady Digwell!" "Yes, corrupting" retorted Lady Digwell calmly taking off her long gloves, what a horrid alluring dangerous voice. "Leave him to me for an hour dear Mademoiselle, at the end of that time you will find him quite changed, quite amenable, quite docile. I assure you."

I was terrified out of my wits. This woman would massacre me, tear me limb from limb or worse, corrupting! what did she mean by corrupting? I shuddered and shrank at the dreadful import of the word.

"I hope so," replied Mademoiselle, with a laugh as she left the room.

"Oh Mademoiselle, Mademoiselle, pray, pray, pray don't leave me, don't leave me to her" I entreated but Mademoiselle only laughed again and shut the door behind her. I heard her also shut the door of her own room and with that sound all hope left me and I stood at bay with my unknown fate in the power of that monster of a woman before me.

"Now then young gentleman, no nonsense with me," and she walked up to me and gave me a cuff which made my head sing, and made me silly.

"I love disciplining boys—lie down on that bed" she said, having unstrapped me, and glancing at me; I quailed under her eye and obeyed.

She immediately began playing with her hand all over my body tickling me in short—she tickled and played with my testicles and slipped her hand frequently between my legs. Like a moth round a candle her hand moved about round and round and at length entered itself at my back, my bottom. I hoped she would spare me, I had never been touched there. She did not spare me. She pressed her hand in and fingered my arse the existence of which I had hoped to conceal from her. I groaned and cried but she forcibly held me down on my face and at length, horror of horrors, inserted her finger well into me. I could not control myself, I wept bitterly I felt so utterly outraged. She continued torturing me in this manner for several minutes, my feelings stronger than I had ever yet experienced them quickly became overpowering. I could not control them—throb—throb—throb— went the engine in front more violently than under Mademoiselle's manipulation; that was nothing; it was so awful to have that woman's hand up my bottom, one finger inside me. I could have done anything to escape the degradation.

"I hope you enjoy your punishment," she said, moving her finger inside me. "You see I know how to punish an obstreperous boy. No woman has punished you like this yet, eh? It is very real sound punishment, is it not? You would not be able to hold your head up before me, or your cousin, or any of them when you are taken down to the drawing-room presently and I tell them how I have punished you Miss!"

"Miss!" how fearful!

"Yes Miss."

Worse was to come. After quite a quarter of an hour of this treatment, by which time I was reduced to the lowest depths of shame, the creature turned me on my back put me face upwards under her loathsome legs, and bending over me still keeping her hands on my bottom, and her fingers busy about and in my rear, put my excited wet organ into her mouth, bit it playfully and then sucked it. Do what I could the consequences may easily be imagined and soon happened and in her mouth. She repeated the operation after a few minutes I felt as though she were sucking the life out of my poor mangled body.

At last she left me utterly overcome.

Returning from Mademoiselle's room in a few minutes she wrapped a peignoir about me having first put on my vest and the corset which she laced most severely, and took me down to the drawing room.

There were Mademoiselle, Beatrice, Barbara, and Lady Edith.

"I have properly punished this saucy minx,

dear Mademoiselle."

"How?" said they all.

"He has had to submit to having my fingers up his arse."

"Oh!" said they all, growing a fiery red.

"And has had to disgrace himself, his affair has been in my mouth!"

"Oh the wretch, the beast!"

"Go to your room, you horrid creature." said Mademoiselle, "you loathsome thing, and remember what you will have to do, it will be fit employment for you now, you are good for nothing else."

I could not speak a syllable.

Hating myself, I went, I covered my face with my hands and threw myself on the floor. I dared not even think. I wept bitterly and for a long time.

Lisette found me in this condition when she came about half past ten to put me into Mademoiselle's bed naked. I was compelled to huddle myself together at its foot underneath the clothes. Mademoiselle presently sprang in, she caught me between her naked legs and forced my face up to her bottom. It was perfumed, and like velvet. I kissed her with some reluctance. I could not to save my life insert my tongue.

After some minutes, perhaps half an hour of persuasion, forcible persuasion on her part, and attempts and failure on mine, she lost her patience.

She got out of bed, bound my hands and seizing a new birch lashed me with it till I was mad with pain.

"Will you? Will you?" she asked at each stroke, "obey my orders? I shall lash you until you do, till you bleed, I shall flog you, I shall till you—you must—you must, you must kiss my bottom, you must kiss my arse, you must insert your tongue as you did into me in front"—lash, lash, lash—"you must kiss it just as much."

And she turned me over and put my face under her. I made some vain attempts with my tongue.

"Very well if you will promise I shall not birch you any more, if you don't I shall, and besides will hand you over to Lady Digwell and tell her how you have behaved and get her to make you do it to her." I screamed "Mademoiselle." I would make this sacrifice for her to escape such torture and such a fate, and I gave the promise.

"You will not make me do it to Lady Digwell?

"Not if you are good and obey me" she replied smiling.

I jumped into bed. Mademoiselle followed me. She put her soft bottom against my face, and a leg across my head.

I shut my eyes. I soon found what I had to kiss. She placed her own hands on my rear. Some effort and great determination was needed which made it all the worse. I forced my tongue in endeavouring to be unconscious of what I was doing. I had my reward. Mademoiselle appeared to be transported beyond herself and her mood entirely altered towards me.

For ten minutes she kept me in obdurate confinement so rigidly pressed against her flesh that I breathed with great difficulty.

What I had to kiss was firmly and uncompromisingly forced against my mouth and my nostrils were unheeded in the plump cushions warm and yielding protecting it.

The pleasure of being under a girl's bottom was spoilt by the beastly office I was compelled to discharge but there was no escape.

What a tight, tough bottom of a thing it was; so unlike the neighbouring organ which distented itself easily with complaisance. Here there was no help. If I did not do it myself and set deliberately and persistently to work it would not be accomplished. The position and the task set me strangely united pleasure with pain.

The task was a decided punishment. There was no escape, Mademoiselle's hand at the back of my head held it immovably; her body wriggled against my face as my tickling her with my tongue gave her increasing excitement. Her anger gradually melted away and her mood became inexpressibly tender. She caressed and played with me in front, she uttered soft sounds of intense love sickness, inarticulate but expressive of a high degree of pleasure. She however continued to punish me severely with the most disagreeable portion of her body. At last I discovered an aperture. My tongue entered the folds of muscle. Mademoiselle increased the pressure and gave a final wriggle—a wave of passion passed over me and I became utterly reckless, I opened my mouth as widely as I could make it, and by degrees, it made its way in.

It was crushed by the construction of the sphincter but there was no mercy, I had for my sins to force it into my governess's bottom (the idea that it was a lady's asphyxiated me at the moment) I got it well in and wagged it about as much as its strength and length permitted, inside.

Mademoiselle at this consummation gave a little scream of delight and appeared perfectly furious with the excitement occasioned her. She moved her hands over my head and lovingly about my body she spoke gentle words to me and called me by endearing names. She pressed my hand against herself in front and it was presently deluged with the physical expression of her emotion.

It is so that ladies confess the power of love upon them. It was impossible to keep my tongue more than two or three minutes where it was. When the crisis had occurred however Mademoiselle was content. I was glad of it for although much excited myself I felt very sick. I was sure I should get typhus or typhoid or putrid fever, but I tasted nothing except extreme bitterness. Mademoiselle told me with limpid eyes over which the lids drooped very heavily to go and wash.

I had done enough. She then recalled and clasped me to her bosom saying that I was her own obedient good boy, and added archly that whenever in future I disobeyed she would insist upon apology and full amends to her bottom.

A pleasant conceit and punishment in very truth! To have to kiss the bottom of the mistress one had disobeyed was indeed being literally sat upon for the offence; a very good reason for obedience; a very appropriate and thorough punishment for refractory behaviour; for how could one be disobedient or refractory when reduced to that humiliation and active compliance with a lady's requirements, than which none could be more exacting.

With this terrible penalty hanging over my head I resolved on no account ever to disobey.

The idea of it all excited me to the last degree and I thought gave me a favourable opportunity for communicating my notion to my governess. It seemed to me to be so excessively naughty as to be almost wicked. But what reason now was there for reticence towards one I knew so intimately? My experiences had cured me of mealy mouthedness and reserve. Without making any façon, without scruple therefore, I ventured upon kneading her freely in front. My fondling appeared to have a soothing effect and she abandoned herself with fascinating unreserve.

"Oh Mademoiselle!" I whispered, "how I should like, how I long to put this big thing which longs to be naughty in—here—and to let it tell you there all it feels.

"Do you think I might—do you think it could go in—is it too improper too large" startled at what seemed the immorality of my suggestion and my temerity—"do permit me."

"Of course it would go in—it is made for that—would you like it? so very much?"

Made for it? Here was a revelation. So man could not dispense with woman and this accounted for all her extraordinary dominion over him and was the explanation of all my physical experiences.

"Above all things—above all things here or anywhere."

"So now you are making love to me indeed, why" with a maiden's coyness, "should I give you this great privilege, why should I favour and console that great thing by allowing it to tell all its sensations, communicate all its tender secrets to me?" and she put a dainty limb across me and looked full into my eyes.

"Because I love you, because you love me."

"*L'amour prime le droit.*"

"Oh well, it is a sound argument, but as for being so sure about my loving you, do you not think you are a little conceited?"

"You must let compassion supplement it and cloak my unworthiness!"

"A gallant speech, dear child, and as your governess you have a right to my sympathy in all your little trials and those of the emotions are the most serious."

"You yourself have inspired them, you alone can solace and heal the wounds you have inflicted!"

How delightful it was that she was my governess, how delightful it was that she was older so that in my blind anguish of passion I could confidently and implicitly give myself up to her guidance secure of attaining thereby the fullest felicity. As she intruded her arms and snowy bosom beneath my back on the large pillow my eyes filled with tears of joy. She grasped my body with her legs and drew my mouth near hers at length placed her full ripe lips on mine. I felt nothing now but unalloyed inexpressible rapture. With her hand she gently guided me into her own exquisite body. I sank into her embrace. The ecstasy of reciprocating love overpowered us both—her eyes closed coyly under my gaze; every moment increased my transport and her own. No language was needed, sounds merely represent actions. This was actual love realized, no need to talk of it.

The moment arrived and I became united body, soul and spirit with Mademoiselle. The pains, aches and torments of love vanished as if by magic, a feeling of intense and complete satisfaction stole over my whole being. All my longings, all my desires, all my wishes were accomplished, I was happy beyond the power of language. I wanted nothing, cared for nothing. I possessed all. Clasped in each other's arms, we at length fell asleep.

When the May morning broke, I had been at this time eleven months at Holywell Hall, and the fresh air and sunshine, the scent of the flowers from the garden and birds' songs came streaming into the room, Mademoiselle again permitted me this ecstasy. Without a word, only looking at me most affectionately she sweetly motioned me again to the Paradise in which I had lain all the night. Her silence was eloquent, words would have broken with their roughness the delicate chains that bound us. I was glad she did not speak.

I again tasted her love, her warm soft wet flesh given up entirely and exclusively to me. I loved her with my whole being. She had certainly established a firm physical foundation for this love, but there was a reunion also between our souls.

Mademoiselle Diane d'Erébe had become the world to me. I could not live away from her. She animated creation. My existence began and ended with her.

Notwithstanding during the two years longer that I remained at Holywell Hall she frequently treated me with the old severity. It was seldom and only as a great reward that she permitted me the joys I have vainly attempted to describe. But there was a sweet secret between us, which made her tyranny, tolerable, even delicious; and beside she always kept me in her own hands. She birched me, frequently whipped me, frequently punished and tortured me, but did not have it done by Barbara, Beatrice, Lady Edith or even Lady Digwell. Instead of Barbara's clothes I was now always dressed in my own. Lisette was not permitted to take liberties with me. Subjection was indeed a delight, and I now knew why.

Studies were seriously undertaken, how easy it was to learn from Mademoiselle. The intercourse, the intellectual intercourse we enjoyed possessed so great a charm that study was robed of its labour; it was no longer a burden to the flesh.

Besides my love, confessed, acknowledged and rewarded, filled me with serene content and happiness. Obedience to Mademoiselle became a labour of love. I only rebelled when I wished to apologize, and that I was invariably, and upon each occasion, promptly compelled to do without afterwards receiving the favours accorded my upon the first occasion.

Mademoiselle read Greek with facility, was an

accomplished Latinist, possessed a comprehensive, a philosophical knowledge of history. Gibbon was her favourite writer. She enjoyed the acute and cold satire, the sarcasm and ironical scepticism of his style.

Poor Phyllis I quite forgot. And Laura had been eclipsed. Alas! those happy years are now long passed. They fled too rapidly; the time came for me to proceed to the University. My grief at parting with Mademoiselle was ill assuaged by the prospect of but occasionally seeing her; for I knew I should never again find myself under her sweet sway.

The subject is a painful one to dwell upon.

My distinction at the University was the offering of my soul, of my love to Mademoiselle, but when after a considerable interval, I again saw her she was not, it seemed to me the Mademoiselle Diane d'Erébe that I had known, and yet I do not think she had changed much.

The alteration was in myself. I wondered that I could have ever intended to seek her hand in marriage. It is true she had certainly grown older.

Of all people that she should marry she choose the curate of the parish. We often still correspond but the little wings have wasted away the little god.

I often weep over the grave of my first love. It was sincere.

But although I should have been furious at the curate marrying my Mademoiselle Diane, the Mademoiselle Diane did not seem to be mine.

With a bitter and cruel despair gnawing my

heart I came to the conclusion that after all love was but a dream, but an imagination, and so I resolved to avoid matrimony.

The sequel will show that for a long period I did so, and even ultimately I was married and did not marry. My last chapter of all however I remember will show that I am not such an absolute heretic or sceptic as may be supposed from what I have just said. But then it treats of the present; it is up to date in one sense although perhaps not in the general sense.

Ah! my first love—well I won't waste more words on the subject. And what about Laura? Might it have been her? Is first love only the first time?

One observation more and it is that however shocking my education may seem to the sensibilities, yet it did me an infinity of good for I should never have attained the knowledge and distinction, the self possession and the mental freedom I did attain without Mademoiselle and her system, whatever may be thought of her and it.

It will possibly be alleged that the mischief there would probably have been worse without the addition of the education which had developed and freed my mind and the learning I had been induced to acquire. The slap of placing me under a governess was wise and very beneficial. Many a young man would I believe vastly improve under feminine rule and discipline who without it goes to the dogs.

However the reader shall judge for himself when he has perused my whole history. In the meantime let him contemplate this tail piece.

Two figures, a youth and a maiden, have caught Cupid by the wings, of which they vainly attempt to deprive him. When they remove their hands, he will fly. The youth is myself, but I will not say that the damsel is Mademoiselle Diane d'Erébe, for an unholy doubt harasses and torments me. Possibly it should represent only the girl whoever she might be with when for the first time he ousted and succeeded in catching the tenant. This though I will not, I do not, believe. A child would have incarnated and immortalised our love. It was none the less a reality because not incarnated. I shall meet it again; where the emotions of the soul live long and have their being.

THE END

Excerpt:

Stays and Gloves

Figure-Training and Deportment by Means of the Discipline of Tight Corsets, Narrow High-Heeled Boots, Clinging Kid Gloves, Combinations, etc., etc.

by

Lord Kidrodstock

1909

Forthcoming
Birchgrove Press
2011

STAYS and GLOVES

CHAPTER I

I had just reached the age of ten when my father died. At this period we lived in a nice-looking house. But the quarter bears that stamp of poverty which is all-prevailing in the East-End of London. The dwelling is in Shepherdess Walk, close to the City Road.

I went regularly to the district-school and was reputed a bad scholar. The master was kind, although we found his haughty manner very trying. He was content to go through his lessons. If he asked a question or made an observation, he did so briefly, in a manner devoid alike of politeness and roughness. Never did I see him in a temper. He rarely rebuked and struck more rarely still. On these latter occasions, it was a rap with the ruler upon the fingers as he passed. And he did not pause either to console or to reprimand the weeping child whom he had hit.

The death of my father brought about great changes. Without being rich, we had been comfortably off. My mother was always ill at ease in this quarter of poor people, she with her prettiness, refinement and distinction. She was also still young, for she was not quite eighteen years old when she brought me into the world.

After my father's funeral, my first recollection is the visit of a gentleman who was on very familiar terms with my mother and me although I had never seen him previously. After my father's death he was a daily caller. Sometimes he took my mother on his knees arid kissed and caressed her. At these moments the faces of both were very red. At times she would seize hold of his arm and with a movement of her eyes make signs towards me. But the gentleman would laugh and reply:

"Absolute nonsense! What does that young innocent know of the fires of love?"

I disliked him and yet I was always glad of his visits, for he always brought me a toy or some sweets and sometimes both. Indeed he was not above playing with me. But — though whether inadvertently or purposely I do not know — he made me feel quite queer: for his manner of touching me as he raised me from the ground or as he rolled me over and over made feel ashamed and unnerved.

I no longer went to school.

The three of us would step into a very beautiful carriage drawn by two horses, and in Mr. Joe Baker's (for such was his name) fine turn-out, we would drive to the West-End, to Portland Place, to a beautiful mansion belonging to him and containing a vast number of grooms and maid-servants.

All the latter were pretty. They were both fair and dark, gentle and proud, but all were remarkable. They were not dressed as English domestics usually are, except that they wore, as is customary, the little linen cap, so stylish, light and charming. The other parts of their costume were of a picturesque nature. All wore aprons of brilliant, coloured silk and a dress with no sleeves. On their hands and arms were exceedingly tight gloves of glazed kid, coloured black or dark brown, and very long, reaching above the elbow. I was struck by this particular feature in their costume. It seemed strange that humble maid-servants should wear such valuable gloves. My little brain, much puzzled, sought a solution of this mystery, but with no success. The events which I shall relate threw light upon the matter for me as they will not fail to do for the reader. For the time being, I could not get beyond this simple conclusion: that Mr. Joe Baker must posses a vast fortune if he could clothe his servants so sumptuously.

As I have said, we used to leave our house in Shepherdess Walk in the carriage and Mr. Baker would come himself to fetch us, but at times it was merely the carriage which would drive up to our door. We would lunch and dine with Mr. Baker who would not fail to remark at table that I was exceedingly ill-mannered, yet without giving the least suggestion as to how I should correct myself. His observation, always accompanied on his part with smiles and affability, did not fail to cover me with con-fusion. I sought to discover in what respect I was bad-mannered, but in vain and I finished by asking Mr. Baker what he found amiss in my behaviour. His sole reply was a fit of laughter, when my mother became greatly annoyed. She boxed both my ears and I remember that the pain was nothing to me as compared with my sense of the injustice of her act. I wept with grief and vexation, bursting into hysterical sobs, which exhibition had for result my being sent away to finish my luncheon in the servants' hall.

A maid came to lead me away and see after my meal. She was tall, dark, and stout with very big eyes looking blackly out from under heavy brows. Her lips were red and full, and the suspicion of a moustache was visible. Her thick arms carried without a single wrinkle the black, glazed kid gloves. She took me by the hand. I stamped and resisted, but in vain; she took me away without effort. I was, however, in a terrible passion due to my mother's injustice which I had never previously experienced. I let myself fall to the ground and tried to kick.

The maid took me in her arms. I struggled and cried, saying that I wanted to leave the house immediately. I tried to bite her. But we were already in the hall. Here she handled me as Mr. Baker had done, but with more insistence. The sensation due to the contact of the kid glove immediately calmed my anger. I became at once quite tractable, my mind being filled with a strong desire to obey this tall girl and do everything she wished. It was at this moment that she smiled at me pleasantly.

In the servants' hall, as she watched me eating, she frowned from under her heavy brows. Then in a rough voice, she ordered me to cease eating bread. To tell the truth, I was in the habit of eating a great deal of bread, far more than is eaten in England where they take scarcely any. I used at that time to stuff my mouth with bread between the courses and consequently had little appetite for meat and vegetables. My father had only laughed and used often to say that "in my gluttony for bread I was a true Frenchman." I repeated this saying of my father to the maid, whose name was Betsy.

She shrugged her shoulders disdainfully and replied that my father was a poor sort of man who had brought me up badly, or rather who had not brought me up at all, but all was going to change now.

My lassitude of a few minutes before was succeeded by a mood of excessive irritation. Her contempt for my poor dear father whom I so sincerely mourned, I found unbearable. I burst into bitter reproaches of Betsy's cruelty, assuring her that my father had been worth Mr. Baker a thousand times over. She roughly told me to hold my tongue, adding:

"You are an impertinent little boy!"

"No!" cried I. "It is you who are insolent. You have no right to speak of my father except with respect, as a servant should."

She turned pale at the insult and directed so terrible a look at me that I immediately regretted my imprudence.

Then appearing to recover herself, she rejoined:

"Not another word! Instead of gossiping, you would do well to eat this nice piece of underdone meat. It is better than stuffing yourself with bread."

So I tried to leave the bread alone, but so strong is habit that I began eating it again absent-mindedly, filling my mouth gluttonously.

"You disgust me!" said Betsy. "You perfect little gormandizer!"

The meal was however, at an end. She showed me fruits and jam and then replaced them in the cupboard without offering them to me. She said that as a punishment for my impertinence, I should be deprived of dessert. Then she came and sat close to me, putting one arm round my neck and patting my face in an affectionate way. I do not know if it came from her arm or from her glove, but the perfume which entered my nostrils intoxicated me.

"Your father ought to have whipped you," she said.

I made no answer. She continued. "Have you ever been whipped?"

"Never!"

"Well! You are going to be then! You deserve punishment."

"Really?" said I, escaping from her. "And who's going to whip me, I should like to know?"

"I am!"

She had already caught me in her powerful arms. I struggled, kicked, threatened, tried to bite and scratch her, without appearing to make the least effect upon her. This woman of thirty was very strong and had no difficulty in getting the better of a poor little child of my age. She gave me some sound cuffs on the ears which made me giddy. Then she put me down on the ground so violently that I almost had a fall. She gave me this order:

"Unbutton your clothes!"

"What?" said I, in astonishment.

"Take your knickerbockers down!"

I was about to obey her mechanically, when I was seized with a transport of anger and began stamping and shrieking. She then said:

"You refuse to obey me?"

"Why yes! I do refuse... You must be mad."

"Very well!" she replied. "You shall pay for this impertinence and for your rudeness at lunch at the same time."

In the twinkling of an eye, her quick fingers, in spite of her gloves, had unbuttoned my knickerbockers which she then proceeded to pull down to my heels. Pulling up my shirt, she laid me across her knees and gave me a very sound spanking which made me bellow and shriek. The slaps fell thick and loud while she cried to me:

"Shriek away, my young gentleman! Shriek as much as you like. No one will come to your aid. Presently I'm going to give you good reasons for crying yourself hoarse. That I promise you!"

After soundly spanking me, she set me on my feet again and told me to open the drawer of the sideboard, take the birch-rod which I should see there and bring it to her. Instead of obeying her, I rushed away, as she released me, nearly falling at full length on the floor on account of having my knickers down, and took refuge in the farthest corner of the room. With my face turned to the wall, I began to cry bitterly.

"One! Two!... Are you going to obey?"

I trembled at her voice and sobbing more than ever, as though my head was splitting, went to the sideboard. On finding the drawer, I was seized with a new fit of passion and crying worse than ever, took refuge once more in my corner.

She got up, seized the rod herself, and holding me by the ear, led me back to the chair. She then made me go down on my knees in front of her, and holding my head between her knees, she flogged me during long minutes, paying no heed whatever to my tears and entreaties.

"Another time I shall flog you till the blood comes, naughty little rascal! It's the only way to make you mend your ways."

I shrieked, rolling on the ground. She told me to get up. I did not want to listen to another word and lay where I was. Leaning down over me, she inflicted a caress on me, which far from calming me, unnerved me more than ever and made me fall into a state of dull stupefaction.

She dried my eyes, washed my face in cold water and led me back to the drawing-room, where ready to die of wretchedness and grief, I seated myself apart from my mother and Mr. Baker who at first paid no attention to me. It was only after some minutes that my mother glanced at me attentively, saying:

"Look at him! One would think he had been crying."

Mr. Baker, who was seated in a revolving arm-chair with his back towards me, slowly wheeled round. In his turn, he gazed at me, but in a contemptuous way which set my heart thumping. He laughed sarcastically, and then suggested:

"Let him alone. It only makes him conceited when attention is paid to him. I quite understand what it is. He's been impertinent and Betsy has punished him. She has a heavy hand — the wench!"

His face bore a strange expression as he said those words, and it seemed to me as though he were menacing me. My mother must have understood the words in the same way, for I saw her redden and lower her head in confusion. Rising to her feet, she looked at Mr. Baker apprehensively; so, at any rate, I interpreted her glance. Later, when the course of events had brought me light, I remembered that my childish intuition had not been at fault. My boyish mind did not easily reach this conclusion which I found very astonishing. I was so absorbed in my reflections on the matter that I trembled at hearing myself addressed in a stern voice by Mr. Baker.

"Well! your wits have gone wool-gathering? Listen to me and have done with your blue devil's stare! It is important that you should hear what I say to you. I have known your mother for a long time. She was my mistress during your father's lifetime."

My mother tried to interrupt him.

"Oh! Joe..." was all she could say.

As for me, without precisely understanding the meaning of the words, I saw that they contained something insulting to my father's memory and in my grief I burst into a storm of sobs.

My mother cried, too, and ran to me to take me in her arms, I avoided her and as she ran to me to take me in her arms, I put out my arms to push her away.

Mr. Baker again burst into a hard unpleasant laugh.

"Ha! Ha! He doesn't want you to come near him. Leave him alone, or I shall ask Betsy to take you into the Punishment Room. As for you young man, this is what I have got to say to you. I have decided to marry your mother. The ceremony will take place next week. But I should be ashamed to show my friends a big boy so badly brought up as you. So you won't take part in the rejoicings. As your education has been horribly neglected and you cannot imitate your father's good manners because he hadn't got any, it is high time for me to think of crushing your stubborn will and teaching you how to behave in society. I have got money, and I am quite willing to spend a large sum in so praiseworthy an object. That is the reason why you will go to school tomorrow. You will be very comfortable there, for the establishment of Mrs. Flayskin is well managed. I may even say that it is a perfectly aristocratic boarding-school where you will meet with the heirs and heiresses to the greatest titles of the United Kingdom and to the biggest fortunes of America. If you behave yourself well and make progress; in a word, if the mistress declares herself satisfied with your conduct, you will pass your holidays with us. I don't think you are a bad child. You love your mother. That is good. Only, in your own interest, you must bend your unruly spirit. While there is yet time, you must uproot your instincts of revolt. You understand then? To morrow you will leave the house. Betsy will take you. Come, give me your hand and let us be friends."

But already, like one distraught, shrieking in despair; my whole body convulsed with sobs, I had made a rush for the door wishing to flee this accursed house for ever. My idea was to gain the street and then go on foot to our own house to find once more the abode where my beloved father had died. Through the tears obscuring my sight I recognised Betsy. My childish fits were doubled in vain. They were powerless against those strong arms cased in black kid.

No sooner had I reached the outer door, than I felt myself caught in a vigorous grip.

CHAPTER II

Mrs. Flayskin, or, more correctly, Lady Flayskin, for by her marriage with Lord Flayskin she had entered the highest ranks of the English nobility — the class which has given the country its most illustrious soldiers and politicians — Lady Flayskin, then, was of American origin. Her beauty was of the American style which is often somewhat grotesque; that is to say, that while the general effect was pleasing, the details were defective. Her eyes were too deeply set and too far apart, one from the other. Her nose was too broad at the top and turned up at the tip like a bird's beak. Her appearance greatly impressed me, nevertheless. She was tall, she spoke softly and slowly, and could at will give a languid intonation to her words as befitted a blonde beauty.

When Betsy and I entered the room into which we were shown, we found Lady Flayskin, and with her a gentleman who appeared to me even more rigid and starched than Mr. Baker. By his nasal twang I took him to be an American. I was right. In New York he was a personage of note, for he was there actively engaged in the organisation of societies for the prevention of vice and assiduously busied himself with the private lives of other citizens.

He had also succeeded, thanks to his obstinate importunity, in getting the government to decide that it was the duty of magistrates to exercise astringent supervision over the morals of the people and by the severity of punishments inflicted, to check every deviation from the narrow path of purity calculated to set a bad example.

In his present surroundings, he seemed entirely at his ease and quite at home.

When we entered, he addressed Lady Flayskin. After fixing on me his round, cold light grey eyes he remarked:

"Another pupil for you?"

"Why, certainly."

"He appears to me to be in need of supervision."

"All have to be controlled and punished."

"I think so too!"

"Oh! you and I know that we have long held identical opinions."

"That does us credit. In truth, the world would be a better place than it is if everyone was imbued with the conviction that youth requires moral training."

"Which only the rod can impart."

"Very true."

This conversation to which I listened openmouthed was not reassuring.

I had already tasted the whip as applied by the rough hand of Betsy and did not feel tempted to renew its acquaintance. My little posterior still smarted from the whipping of the day before.

After Betsy had explained who I was, and had hugged me in her big arms, covering my face the while with a rain of kisses in effusiveness which I found more astonishing than affecting, Lady Flayskin entrusted me to the keeping of an under-mistress who had just entered the room in hurried response to the summons of an electric hell.

The latter was a thick-set dumpy woman of incredible mobility. Even when she was not speaking and was sitting in her chair, all her body moved: eyes, nose, lips, and bust. She had movements for asking questions, for doubting, for hesitating and for signifying approval. Yet this was not through lacking a fine large tongue, as I was able to notice. During the few moments required to conduct me through the corridor to the class-room assigned to me, she found means to tell me a great many most curious things. Among other items of information, she told me that Lady Flayskin was a person of real distinction, a typical member of the aristocracy. That the profession of school-mistress was with her nothing less than a sacred call. That as I could easily see, she had no need whatever to undertake occupation of any kind. That thank God! — the late regretted Lord Flayskin had left his wife an immense fortune. Then she broke off suddenly and enquired if I wore stays?

I was much surprised at the question and although the circumstances of my present position were by no means of a sort to incite me to gaiety, the idea that I could have stays on, made me burst into laughter.

Immediately this person who had been all smiles and pleasant chat, changed countenance with a suddenness which inspired me with terror. My laughter was choked in my throat. With nostrils distended, her eyes full of menace, the stout little woman shook my arm roughly, pulling and pushing me here and there as though I had been the handle of a pump and she had resolved to pump out of me my crowning irreverence.

"Little wretch! What possesses you to make you laugh like that? If you are not accustomed to stays those I am going to put on you will make you suffer. We shall then see if you are still in a laughing mood."

We had reached the class-room. We found no pupils therein. All were in the dormitory, it being the time when girls and boys had to wash their hands before appearing at table. But the mistress under whose orders I was to study was still there. She proved to be a narrow strip of a woman with straight tow-coloured hair, as angular and sparing of gesture as my fat, dark-haired and black-eyed conductress was rotund and vivacious.

"Mrs. Stuart", said the dumpy woman, bowing pleasantly to the thin one, "this is young Sanderson of whose coming you have already heard. Shall he sit down to table as he is, or do you wish him to be dressed like the others?"

"What a question!" replied the other with a shrug of her lean shoulders. "Certainly it is unfitting that he should be different from the others. It would be notorious disorder and nothing less. Has not Lady Flayskin given you any instructions on the matter?"

"She must have forgotten. I neglected to ask her for precise instructions."

"Then the duty devolves upon me. Go immediately to the store-room and get things to fit him. If luncheon is finished, he will have to eat by himself, that's all. But I am resolved that he shall not mingle in those outrageous clothes with the pupils. It would be a case of the wolf in the fold!"

I did not understand in the least what was required of me; but with feelings more affected than I can tell, I quietly followed my conduct-ress who now took me to the outfitting establishment. Here a vast number of little girls' dresses were hung up by hooks, while boxes containing boots with high heels were arranged in their order of size upon the shelves. There were drawers containing glazed kid gloves. Others contained petticoats, dressing-jackets and pairs of stays. Then again there was a little girls' drawers department. In short, it was a typical wardrobe.

She began by taking my measurements with a great deal of vivacity. Her hands went hither and thither over my body and irritated my nerves. I became ill at ease and ashamed. She noticed my confusion and only laughed.

She quickly took my clothes off and found fault with the cleanness of my body, although Betsy had washed me all over that same morning. She therefore took me into an adjoining room which proved to contain a bath. I was plunged into the water and abundantly soaped. Her hands affected me indescribably. She seemed to put both malice and craft into her movements. When I appeared to her sufficiently white and clean, she dried me, delaying the operation longer than appeared necessary, and then led me back again to the clothes store.

She began by rigging me out in a little sleeveless chemise such as girls wear. Then she put on my legs very long stockings of black spun silk. After that, she decked me out in a little girl's drawers and a pair of stays which she tight-laced with all her strength, almost preventing me from breathing. The stiff whalebones then proved painful. But this physical discomfort was as nothing in comparison with the shame I felt at being thus dressed up in a fashion so little in accordance with my sex. Like all children of my age, I was not a little proud of being a boy. It seemed to me that this costume changed me undoubtedly into a girl.

I was not at the end of my martyrdom...

BIRCHGROVE PRESS
Flagellant & Libertine Erotica

Birchgrove Press specializes in producing new print and e-book editions of pre-1950s writings on sexual flagellation in English. Original editions of many of the books that we offer are difficult to obtain and are highly sought after. We are especially proud to offer new editions of rare Victorian flagellant texts such as *The Mysteries of Verbena House*, *Experimental Lecture by Colonel Spanker*, and *The Quintessence of Birch Discipline*. Birchgrove Press also produces new editions of libertine literature. We have published *Venus in the Cloister*, *The School of Venus*, *The Dialogues of Luisa Sigea*, and Isidore Liseux's translation of the Marquis de Sade's *Justine* (1791), *Opus Sadicum*, for example. For a full list of titles and formats, please visit our website:

www.birchgrovepress.com.